"I know how to love!"

Blake made the admission grudgingly, through gritted teeth. "You've taught me that."

Joy—pervasive, euphoric—sang through Jamie. She took a step toward him. "Then all we have left is the laughing. You smiled once in the rain. Maybe you can do it again. Tilt your face up to the sky—"

"Forget the damn rain." He pulled her into his arms, and on his face was a look that took the breath from her body. "I have one last question for the teacher.... What are you like to make love to, Jamie? Sweet and shy, as if it were the first time? Or passionate and hot . . . as if it were the last?"

Then he kissed her as if he meant to find out.

SHIRLEY LARSON
is also the author
of this novel in
Temptation

WHERE THE HEART IS

Laughter in the Rain

SHIRLEY LARSON

MILLS & BOON LIMITED
ETON HOUSE, 18–24 PARADISE ROAD
RICHMOND, SURREY TW9 1SR

First published in Great Britain in 1987 by
Mills & Boon Limited, Eton House, 18–24 Paradise Road,
Richmond, Surrey TW9 1SR

© Shirley Larson 1987

ISBN 0 263 75990 3

21–0288

Printed and bound in Great Britain by
Cox & Wyman Ltd, Reading

1

I SHOULDN'T BE HERE. I don't belong. . . .

"Where is he, Miss Gordon? Where is he?"

Jamie Gordon smiled down at the nine-year-old anxious face turned up to her. "Well, he's probably waiting in the plane for everyone to get their things and get out of his way so he can charge down the aisle and come running through the door to you," she said, and prayed it was the truth. Brimming with anxious anticipation, Blake Lindstrom's daughter looked younger and more vulnerable than ever, waiting for her father to deplane.

Don't disappoint her, Blake Lindstrom. Whatever you've suffered, whatever you've been through, don't disappoint her. Not now. . . .

Jamie hadn't wanted to be a part of the family group waiting at the airport to meet the man who'd been taken hostage six months earlier. She was Jenny's teacher, and she didn't belong there with Jenny and Drew, Lindstrom's cousin. This was a private time, a time they should be together without an outsider. But Jenny had begged her to come, and how could she refuse when those large brown eyes looked at her so pleadingly?

She'd been drawn to Jenny's shyly quiet charm last fall during her first few weeks in the South Dakota school, and when Blake Lindstrom had been taken hostage in the early part of December, Jamie had been invited by the family to spend Christmas with Jenny to ease the child's pain at being separated from her father. Now, in April, six long months after Blake Lindstrom had been captured, she was much closer to the girl than she had been then.

Her affection for Jenny was one reason she stood in the Sioux Falls airport today, but there was another, more disquieting one. There had been rumors about Blake Lindstrom, disquieting rumors. If they were true...he was not the same man he had been when he left.

"If I'd known there was going to be this big a turnout to meet my cousin, I would have made popcorn and set up a concession stand, made a little profit while I was waiting."

Drew Lindstrom's teasing tone wasn't, Jamie decided, loud enough to carry any farther than her ears, but it still made her uncomfortable. Which was unusual. Drew was known for his sense of humor. Everyone liked him. He was endowed with charm as well as striking good looks, and he had that quality that was as rare as gold these days, the ability to put people at ease. Quite the opposite of his cousin.

The whole airport seemed to resonate with tension, most of which emanated from Jenny. In a few minutes, Lindstrom would be stepping into the lounge where they were.

Jamie put her hands on Jenny's shoulders, whether to comfort Jenny or to contain her own apprehensions, she wasn't sure. That slim, immature body was poised for action like an arrow drawn by a bow. Yet the girl was unnaturally still.

Already, at her tender age, Jenny had learned disappointment. There had been rumors of her father's release for many long weeks before the rumors were confirmed by the major television networks. But even afterward there had been delays, until Jenny had grown drawn, tautly unhappy, afraid to believe her father really was coming home.

But now at last, the day had come. The plane carrying Blake Lindstrom had landed at the airport, and Jenny was minutes away from being reunited with her father.

There was a flurry of activity near the door. Jamie felt her throat tighten. Right at that moment, she wanted to gather her young pupil close and hold her, protect her from yet another hurt. Jenny waited to pour love over her father like oil from a deep, bottomless well. Would he be capable of receiving it?

Despite the fact that Rock Falls was a small town, Jamie had seen Blake Lindstrom only once before in her life, and he hadn't appeared to be a warm, loving man. Early last fall he'd driven into the small town of Rock Falls, which was nestled on the prairie forty miles south of Sioux Falls. He'd been scheduled for the required parent-teacher meeting with Jamie. The conference had not been a success. Lindstrom had made Jamie feel as if she were wasting her time and his. His eyes had been cold, his manner icy. Jamie had attributed his coolness to the fact that he'd been recently divorced. At the time her sympathies had been entirely with his former wife. What would this chilly man be like after spending six months as a hostage?

Then he came through the door.

"Dad!" Jenny shrugged out from under Jamie's restraining hands and dashed to her father. He leaned down and swept her up to his heart, wrapping his arms around her as if he meant never to let her go. In the flurry of flashbulbs that went off, Blake Lindstrom's tortured face was forever caught for posterity.

Jamie felt light-headed with relief. He'd missed his daughter as much as she'd missed him, and he was man enough not to hide it. The beauty of that lean, cynical countenance, brilliant with a joy and relief so acute that it might have been mistaken for anguish, moved her deeply.

He closed his eyes, and an oddly graceful hand came up and cupped the back of his daughter's head, his fingers threading through the black hair that matched his own, his arms enclosing her in the protective cradle of his body.

Then, as if he remembered where he was, he opened his eyes and looked over the girl's shoulder into the throng pressing around them. His height made him tower above the crowd, and Jamie felt he was looking directly at her. For one long, unending instant he stared at her, seeming to see every worry she had about him, all her anxious thoughts about this first meeting with Jenny.

The look of anguished joy vanished as if wiped away. In its place came one that might have been etched in steel. His eyes were so icy that they looked as if every emotion had been erased from them.

A flashbulb went off in his face, so close that his pupils reacted to the blast of light. Blake turned, and it was then that Jamie knew the rumors had been true. There was a dark scar on the right side of his cheek.

There was a gasp here and there and murmurs of distress. "Get the hell out," he growled at the hapless photographer. "Go pick over somebody else's bones. You've plucked at mine long enough."

His tone would have frozen running water, and even the hardened photographer stepped back a pace. Blake's voice matched his eyes . . . and there was no human warmth in either of them.

"My God," Drew murmured in her ear.

For a moment Jamie had the urge to run and snatch Jenny from Blake Lindstrom's arms. That scar told its own story. He'd been through hell. But how much had he changed during his captivity? Was Jenny safe with him? Yet he held her so tenderly. He'd had a terrible experience, yes, but he'd certainly greeted his daughter with open arms.

She was imagining all this. She had to be. He was a man who'd been under great strain, nothing more.

Blake Lindstrom stood and buried his scarred face in his daughter's hair, and in that moment he looked like a starving man having his first taste of a banquet.

Jamie's heart twisted with sudden, empathetic pain. "He has a right to be ... annoyed. Can't you do something? Show a little cousinly concern and run interference for him."

Drew, as light-haired as his cousin was dark, folded his arms and lifted an eyebrow at Jamie. "This is the age of equality. You run interference."

Jamie was not surprised. Teaching on the same faculty of a small-town school with Drew for the past year had given her the chance to know him well. Drew was charming, but he was also a bit lazy. He avoided movement and controversy with equal zeal. "And you accuse him of being impossible. You're his match."

Drew shrugged his shoulders, his face bland. "Blood will run true."

She slid away from Drew and headed toward Blake and Jenny, inserting herself between the intrepid members of the press and the man and girl. Amazed at her own boldness, she faced the crowd. "Ladies and gentlemen, you're missing the opportunity to interview the one relative of Mr. Lindstrom's that no one from the press has yet interviewed. He's standing right over there. I'm sure he'd be glad to give you a statement—"

It wasn't much, but heads did turn briefly. She caught Drew's look of ironic congratulation in that instant before she clutched Blake Lindstrom's arm and led him away from the gate and into a small private lounge. They were inside with the door safely shut before anyone realized they were gone.

In that sudden and inexplicably explosive quiet, Lindstrom turned around, Jenny still clinging to his neck.

A wind from the Arctic couldn't have made her feel any colder than the look on Blake Lindstrom's face. All emotion had once again been wiped from those green depths, all feeling obliterated. What remained was a control more complete than she had ever seen. In the warm room, a shiver slithered down her spine.

Not knowing what else to do, she retreated into formality. "I'm very glad you're home safely, Mr. Lindstrom." She wouldn't let herself look at him to see his reaction to her words, and she didn't ask herself why. She knew only a strong urge to escape.

And escape she could. But Jenny... She was leaving Jenny in the arms of this man, a man who looked entirely different from the man he'd been six months earlier. Torn, yet knowing there was nothing she could do to ease her misgivings, Jamie leaned close to Jenny while the girl was still nestled in her father's arms and brushed the girl's cheek with a light kiss. An unmistakably male scent reached Jamie's nose, a darkly masculine scent of clean skin and good cologne and leather, and that was almost a shock. She hadn't expected him to smell so humanly male, so... attractive.

Her own forward motion made the arm circling Jenny nudge Jamie's midriff, and she felt a sudden need to pull back, for her body to reject close contact with him. She made the mistake of glancing up, and when her eyes met his, she knew he'd sensed her instinctive withdrawal. His mouth twisted, not in mockery of her, but as if he understood exactly what she was feeling. Unbelievably, his fingers caught her wrist. His hands were as warm as his eyes were cold.

"Wait a minute."

She had remembered the timbre of his voice, deep and masculine, but now it was even deeper, with a huskiness that might have been caused by his reunion with Jenny.

"I'm sorry." For a second that hard mouth with those chiseled lines around it seemed to soften. "I want to thank you for rescuing us from that zoo out there, but I . . . seem to have forgotten your name."

She forced herself to smile at him and look unperturbed. "With what you've been through, I'm surprised you haven't forgotten yours. I'm Jamie Gordon, and—"

At the sound of her teacher's name, Jenny came to life. "Oh, Miss Gordon. Thank you for bringing me to my dad." The girl lunged for Jamie to hug her. Jamie was captured, caught in an awkward embrace that brought her so close to Lindstrom that she could feel his breath stir her hair. Again she felt that need to back away. She didn't want to touch him, didn't want him touching her. But she couldn't move. She was caught by the girl and the man, Jenny's arms around her neck, Blake's fingers gripping her wrist. "I'm glad my dad's home. Thank you for coming with me."

"My pleasure, honey. See you Monday morning."

Jenny released Jamie, transferring her exuberant embrace to her father's neck. Jamie prepared to step away. Suddenly, surprisingly, Blake Lindstrom tightened his grip on her arm. Shock rippled through her. When she looked past Jenny's dark hair into those icy green eyes, her heart seemed to stop.

He smiled that peculiar half smile, as if he knew exactly what she was thinking. But he didn't release his hold on her. "I want to add my thanks to my daughter's."

He might have been asking for the time of day. "That's not necessary, I—"

"It is necessary...for me." Those green eyes probed and delved and seemed to strip her mind clean of coherent thought. Had she imagined they were cold? She was wrong. For just an instant, as if the sun were shining through the sea, she glimpsed the layers of emotion in those green depths, layers that were dark, hidden, too dangerous to explore . . . or share.

"Thanks accepted," she said, easing her arm out of his grasp, thinking that the highly emotional strain of this man's return must be having more of an effect on her than she'd realized. Her imagination was running wild. Blake Lindstrom was an ordinary man in an extraordinary situation, home after six months of captivity. She'd listened to all the radio reports and knew that of all the hostages, Blake had refused to say anything about his incarceration. Others had been more forthcoming, and in every story Blake had been the hero. Now she saw what a high price heroism carried.

"I know you two have a lot to talk about, so I'll be going. See you Monday, Jenny," she said, and turned quickly, unsure exactly why she felt such an urgent need to escape the piercing regard of those green eyes.

She stepped back out into the main part of the airport, to discover that Drew had neatly disposed of every last member of the press and was waiting for her, leaning indolently against the opening of a small shop that sold souvenirs and books.

"You're very efficient. How did you get rid of them all so quickly?"

"You must give the press more credit, my dear. They have an inborn aversion to people who are boring. All I had to do was convince them I had nothing to offer."

"A difficult task. I'm surprised you managed it."

"My talents are unlimited. The only thing I've ever really failed at is getting you to take me seriously." There was a pause, and then, in the lightest of tones, he said, "And now that my cousin has returned to the familial fold, my chances are less than they were."

"You really do have a vivid imagination."

"Come on, Jamie. There's nothing more appealing to a woman than a bruised and beaten hero. He's even got the wound to prove it."

"I don't find your cousin . . . appealing."

"Then I do have a chance?" He was elaborately casual, and for the first time Jamie began to wonder if he really did mean it.

She turned to face him. "It would serve you right if I took you seriously and asked you to buy me dinner."

"I've always wanted you to take me seriously."

"Yes, and in the next breath you crack a joke." For some reason Drew's words brought back the feel of Blake Lindstrom's fingers around her wrist, and the vivid memory of her need to escape. "Think what being seen with me would do to your go-to-the-devil, gay-blade image."

Something flared in his eyes. "Sometimes it becomes tiresome to be, as Jean Kerr puts it, 'affable, affable, affable.'" His tone was light, just as it always was when he talked in a personal vein. Jamie had never taken him seriously, but now she was beginning to wonder.

Drew was known as the Rake of Rock Falls; it w accurate appellation. What was it about his utter movement that was so sexy? She'd always tho getic men were the sexy ones. Meeting Dre tered all her theories, even while she realized that for some reason, his indolent charm was lost on her.

She was trying to think of something to say that would show him she'd be glad to take him seriously, as a friend, at least, if he would settle for that. But at that moment he said in his usual offhand tone, "Okay, forget it. I can see you've already lost interest. Well, console me and let me walk you to the door. Blake will probably spend the next few minutes closeted with Jenny. I'll tag along with you while I'm waiting for them." With the ease of movement that was characteristic of him, Drew took her elbow. "Other than the obvious change in his physical appearance, how did my estimable cousin seem to you?"

"I really don't know him well enough to make any judgments about his state of mind...although—" her mouth twisted in a wry smile as she remembered the way Blake had talked to the reporters "—he seemed about the same as I remembered him."

"Word is he got roughed up for trying to defend one of the women. Cousin Blake is not used to being pushed around—he's used to doing the pushing. The experience was bound to have an effect on him."

It disturbed her to have Drew voice her unspoken fears. "Not a permanent one, I should think."

"I told him he was crazy to go hounding off to the Middle East to look at new ways of growing food in the desert."

Jamie tilted her head to slant a mocking look at him. "Now that he's back, you surely wouldn't stoop to anything so clichéd as telling the poor man you told him so."

"Jamie." Drew took hold of her arm in a surprising show of energy. "Ride back to the house with me while I drop Blake and Jenny off."

Jamie shook her head. "No, I can't do that. I'd feel...out of place." She put her hand on Drew's shoulder, one soldier bracing another for battle. "'You must needs act out this dismal scene alone, Yorick.'"

"That is misquoted and terrible besides. In addition, there is nothing," Drew drawled, reaching up and dislodging her hand from his shoulder, "I 'must needs' less than being part of an emotional scene that elevates my cousin to a new height, above us mortal men."

"Chin up, old chap." She tapped his chin with her knuckles. "You can do it. I'll see you in school on Monday."

"You wouldn't save me from sinking under the morass of adoration for Blake by coming to the family dinner, I don't suppose. His mother is giving it on Sunday."

Blake's face floated into her mind, disembodied, tormented, scarred and, buried in Jenny's hair, beautiful. On the heels of that vision came the needling thought that she would be happy never to see that face again.

Jamie shook her head. "No, Drew. I'd feel like a fifth wheel. Take heart. You'll survive without me." She stretched up to drop a light kiss on his cheek. "Be brave, little buckaroo."

Only when she'd turned to push the door open did she see that Blake Lindstrom and Jenny had come out of the lounge and were standing there, watching her. The thought crossed her mind that he'd probably been there when she'd kissed Drew. An even more disturbing thought was...she wished he hadn't been. Knowing it hardly mattered, she walked out into the watery sunshine.

LATER, after she'd opened the door to her apartment and stepped inside, Jamie told herself her reactions had been perfectly normal. Every living soul in Rock Falls, all six hundred of them, had been charged up for weeks, watching TV and waiting for Blake's release. For some unknown reason, it had become the custom to cluster in front of the set, drink coffee and eat cherry cheesecake while waiting for the ten o'clock news. Tiki had hosted such a party just a week ago. Poor Blake. Jamie would forever associate his lean face, hidden in shadows and distorted by the TV cameras he was trying to avoid, with the tart, sweet smell of cheesecake with cherries. But could she truly feel sorry for a man with eyes as icy as his? He looked as if every bit of human compassion had been drained from him.

Yet he'd held Jenny like a man determined never to let her go again.

She went over those moments in the airport, the relief she'd felt when Blake had greeted his daughter with such love, the jolt she'd had when she'd first looked into his eyes . . . and the incredible strength of his fingers wrapped around her wrist.

For the past six months, for Jenny's sake, she'd tried to stay detached from the emotional frenzy. Jenny had desperately needed someone to keep a cool head, and Jamie had tried to be that person. But now the strain of waiting was over. Blake Lindstrom was home. Perhaps she was feeling let down after so many months of waiting for Jenny's happy day to come.

She had no idea what Lindstrom's captivity had been like. The reports from the media had said only that the hostages were comfortable. Obviously Blake, at some point in his imprisonment, had been less than comfortable.

She took off her coat and tossed it over the back of the couch, thinking Drew was right. Blake was not the type of man to enjoy being at someone else's mercy. He was a man used to controlling his own destiny. Was Drew right about the other aspect? That Blake would suffer aftereffects from his part in the drama the whole world had watched?

AT THE RANCH, Blake and Jenny walked into the house they called home.

"Blake." His mother's voice quavered.

"Hello, Mom." Her face was brilliant with relief and joy, tears bright in her eyes. He went to her and took her in his arms, holding her tall, slender body close, silently thanking her for her strength. The running of the ranch had fallen to her. She'd had Jed and the hands to help her, and he supposed that his uncle, Thad, had even taken up one or two of the reins again, but she'd had Jenny to care for, as well. He was here now, and he could take the burden of responsibility off her shoulders. "Everything's okay. I'm home."

"I can't—" Her voice was husky with emotion. "I've been so afraid something would happen at the last minute and you wouldn't get here—"

"Nothing happened. I'm here."

"Are you all right?" She leaned back to look searchingly at him, her hands tight on his shoulders.

"I'm fine." His mouth lifted. "Appearances to the contrary." His eyes met hers, asking her not to probe any deeper. Not yet. Not till he'd had time to accept the miracle of being home.

"Can I get you something to eat, some coffee?"

Blake shook his head. "I had something during the flight. How have things been going here?"

His mother's eyes continued to search his face, asking unspoken questions. "Jed kept me in line. The herd is still in the winter pasture." His mother hesitated and then said,

"We've had a couple of incidents of rustling, but we only lost a half dozen head."

"When did it happen?"

"A few weeks ago. We think they did it in the middle of the night."

"Did you tell Clem?" Clem was the county sheriff, a rotund man who was a relentless tracker of poachers.

"Yes, we told him." His mother smiled. "He came out and looked around, but he didn't find much. He doesn't think they'll come back."

"If they know what's good for them, they won't. Where is Jed?"

"This is Saturday," his mother chided him gently. "Jed's day off."

He saw it then, the worry in her eyes, in her wrinkled brow. Damn! Wasn't he man enough to keep his mother from worrying more than she already had? "It must be jet lag," he said in a carefully light tone. "I don't even know what day it is. I feel like—" he looked around at the warm wood paneling, the house he'd built to share with Kim, the fireplace he'd constructed himself stone by stone "—a stranger."

"You're not a stranger. You're home…and we're so glad to have you back."

His mother hugged him again, and when Jenny tugged her father's hand, she was folded into the circle of their arms. Her eyes sparkling with tears, Ruth gave Blake another long look, as if determined to feast her eyes on the sight of the son she'd been afraid she'd never see again. Then, clearly needing a prosaic activity to hide her emotion, she took Jenny by the hand, saying she had milk and cookies ready in the kitchen.

Blake went upstairs, into the bedroom he'd once shared with his wife, Kim. He unpacked, putting away what few things he'd bought with the money he'd borrowed from an aide at the American embassy. He would change clothes, but first he had to take a shower.

After his shower, he dressed. Hot water, clean clothes, boots molded to the shape of his foot. Simple things he had taken for granted. He would never do that again. He would treasure everything that was his to enjoy. Enjoy. Could he learn to enjoy life again? A vision flashed into his brain of a woman with long chestnut hair, a slim, lithe body and darkly expressive eyes the color of a South Dakota sky... eyes that had looked at him as if he were an even stranger specimen of humanity than he felt.

Jamie Gordon was twenty-four years old, idealistic and beautiful. She looked too good to believe. While he... he was thirty-one going on ninety. For the past six months he'd been in close contact with people who were prime examples of what men, and sometimes women, could become when they shed the veneer of civilization. And if he ever forgot where he'd been and what he'd seen, all he had to do was look in a mirror.

The doctor in New York City had recommended plastic surgery as soon as possible. Blake had agreed to scheduling the operation. The doctor had given him top priority, but there was still going to be a two-week waiting period to obtain the operating room. That was fine with Blake. He'd wanted to come home first, see Jenny and check on the ranch.

He muttered a word and stood up. He'd been reasonably good-looking once, he supposed; he'd never really given it a lot of thought. He didn't intend to start now. Physically he was what he was, and for the next two weeks he would remain so. People could look or not look, whichever they pleased. That was their problem, not his.

He crossed to the window to look out over the flat, green lushness of his ranch. Jenny and the land. Those were his first priorities.

Blake left the house and strode across the yard to the barn. Two horses, Jenny's Fair Lady and his own black stallion, Storm, were stabled there. Storm whickered and tossed his head in welcome.

"Hello, boy," Blake said softly, running a caressing hand over the horse's black satin flank, watching the stallion's flesh quiver in response.

This was what he needed, to be home and surrounded by animals and earth. Maybe here, at last, he could forget it all. He saddled up Storm and rode out of the barn, heading for the north range.

All things considered, his stock looked good. They'd had rain earlier in March, too much of it, unusual for South Dakota, bringing the threat of flash floods. His captors had told him about the rains, and when he'd shown concern for his family, they'd used his concern to taunt him. Only after he'd been released had he learned that none of his family had been hurt.

It was a form of torture they used on him over and over, telling him lies. *We're going to kill you tomorrow.... We're going to release you tomorrow.* And the worst of all: *We have agents who know where your family is.*

Blake had learned, no matter what they told him, to disbelieve them. And he'd learned, the hard way, to trust no one. After the incident with the women, someone—he never knew who—had betrayed him. And that betrayal had earned him the scar he was wearing.

He'd been through hell, and he looked it . . . and felt it. The doctor had told him he would feel like this for some time to come, even after his face had been restored virtually to normal.

He finished his rounds of the cattle, more than satisfied. It would be time for roundup in another three weeks, time to bring the calves in for branding and vaccination.

Back in the ranch yard, in the muddy paddock behind the barn, he could see the sagging corner of the barn corral from where he stood. His mouth determined, his body ready for action, he dismounted and struck out toward the machine shed. That corral was the first order of business.

The machine shed was long, drafty, cool and dark. The light bulb over the workbench was burned out, and no one had bothered to replace it. He broke into a cold sweat and swore softly. He'd walked into this machine shed a million times in the dark, but now he couldn't do it without getting sick to his stomach. He groped in the darkness . . . and it was all back. Every last stinking, nightmare memory. . . . *We are leaving you alone now until you are willing to cooperate.*

He stumbled over something lying on the concrete floor, an old horseshoe. The fine edge of control he'd maintained for six months broke. Uttering an oath with heat and precision, he picked up the offending piece of iron and hurled it against the wall.

The shoe hit the corrugated steel and reverberated like a bell. The sound brought him to his senses.

He leaned over the workbench, supporting himself with both hands, palms flat on the scarred wood, his head down, fighting the sickness.

"Daddy! What was that noise?"

Blake braced himself and spun around. Jenny stood in the doorway, her black hair gleaming with a brown sheen in the late afternoon sun, her face smooth and innocent. Not thinking, he said grittily, "I stumbled over a damned horseshoe."

Jenny took a step backward and hunched her shoulders, the habit she'd developed since her mother had left of drawing into herself physically. His mother had told Blake he'd done the same thing as a child. "I'm sorry, Daddy."

The strained, frightened tone made Blake realize what he'd done.

He'd shared a very special rapport with Jenny since the day she was born. One look and he'd fallen in love, and as Jenny had grown, so had his love for her. And now he'd done exactly what the doctor had said he might do. Irrationally, he'd lashed out at the person he loved most. "Honey," he said, going to her and kneeling to gather her into his arms, "it isn't your fault. It has nothing to do with you."

Stricken with a heavy guilt, Blake wiped the tear that hovered at the corner of his daughter's eye and put his finger under her chin to tilt her face to his. "I came in to get the toolbox. How about you helping me fix that corral fence? Or have you forgotten how to fix a fence?"

Jenny's joyous look of forgiveness only drove the nails of guilt deeper into his consciousness.

Back by the corral, with Jenny hovering under his elbow, Blake stripped off his shirt, baring his pale flesh to the May sun. He showed Jenny how to brace the corner pieces of the corral with a chunk of two-by-four, then hold them there while he drove in the nails. He was aware, as he never had been before, of the sunshine beating down on his back, of the light breeze feathering over his skin, of the pleasure he felt because he was working, working on his land. Whenever the constraint of captivity had gotten really bad, especially toward the end, when they'd been promised release and then denied it at the last minute, he'd used the ranch as his talisman.

It had been a ritual. He would close his eyes and picture the ranch, the hot, primary colors of red barn and green grass and blue sky, his cattle moving over the grass, foraging for their food. He'd imagined the ranch in every season, in the fall when it was still hot enough to take off his shirt and the grasshoppers sprang ahead of him as he walked along the fence line; in the winter, when the rusty backs of the cows dotted the snow-covered ground; in the summer, when the smell of hot, drying alfalfa was like perfume and the collie dogs lay beside the cattle shed, their tongues lolling in the heat. But he'd spent the most time thinking about spring, about the peculiar yellow green of fresh grass, and the first clear blue sky of warm weather, with mares' tails for clouds. . . .

Eyes the same cobalt blue of that sky intruded on his consciousness. A woman's eyes . . . and a woman's scent. The scent of a clean, well-groomed woman, with nothing more frightening on her mind than the comfort of a small child.

"Dad? Did you like Miss Gordon?"

Uncanny, small girl children are uncanny. With eyes as brown and wide as a doe's, Jenny stared up at him anxiously.

"Miss Gordon? Your teacher? Yeah, she seems nice." Feeling like a sixteen-year-old boy caught dreaming in school, he took careful aim at a nail, not wanting to miss and hit his thumb.

"You didn't like her last fall."

"Last fall?" He tried to remember and drew a blank. When had he seen her last fall? He asked the question of Jenny.

"You know. You went to see her. For a parent-teacher conference. You were mad 'cause you had to go and mad when you came home. You said you thought she was a typical female."

Had he? Yes, he had. He remembered now. He hadn't wanted to go to school that day because he'd scheduled an appointment with Kim's lawyer in Sioux Falls for the early part of the afternoon. He'd known the meeting wasn't going to be pleasant, and he'd tried to cancel his five o'clock session with Jenny's teacher. She had calmly assured him that he was her last appointment; if he were a few minutes late, she wouldn't mind. She'd rather wait for him than inconvenience several other parents by trying to reschedule his appointment.

When he'd come out of the lawyer's office that afternoon with the realization that the woman he'd married was willing to bargain away her right to see Jenny on a regular basis—if the alimony payments were high enough—he'd wanted to strangle Kim and kick himself for being fool enough to marry her. He hadn't been in the mood to sit down and calmly discuss Jenny's occasional lapses in doing her homework. What had he said? Had he been a tactless fool? Probably he had.

Now he was an ungrateful fool, as well. Of all the kindnesses that people had done for him since he'd regained his freedom, Jamie's quick action at the airport, extricating him from the press, had been the kindest and the most altruistic. She hadn't asked for anything in return; she'd merely greeted him, kissed Jenny and exited gracefully. He had a feeling she did everything gracefully... including hiding her distaste for his scarred countenance.

"It isn't really important for me to like her, is it? You're the one who has to go and sit in the classroom and look at her every day."

"I don't like her," Jenny announced, blinking solemnly in the sunlight like an owl.

Surprised, Blake straightened. "Why not?"

"Because I love her," Jenny said, as if she thought it silly of him to ask. "You don't like someone you love, do you? You never liked Mommy."

How could a nine-year-old kid who hardly looked old enough to string coherent sentences together set up such a verbal mine field? Not so long ago, he'd outtalked and outthought two armed thugs who had drunk too much and had been bent on attacking two of the women hostages. Now his own daughter had him groping for words. But how could he explain love to a child? He didn't understand it himself. He knew he'd never felt that overrated emotion. Not for Kim. He hadn't loved his wife. He hadn't ever loved anyone except his own family. His daughter.

Blake tossed the hammer into the toolbox, knowing it was his absence that had set Jenny to thinking about her mother. How had she felt, losing first one parent and then the other and all within a year's time? According to his mother, Jenny had been restless at nights, but that was all.

"Listen, honey. Your mother and I liked each other once, but—"

"She found somebody she liked better."

"Yes." *That says it all*, he thought grimly, waiting for the punch of pain, the twist of nerves . . . and was amazed to feel nothing. He didn't have to wonder why. In the past six months he'd learned that there were things more important than knowing the woman he'd chosen to be his wife had had no conception of loyalty or integrity.

"Daddy? What was it like . . . where you were?"

He gazed down at his daughter for a long moment. Then he reached out and ruffled her hair. "Remember that time I took you to the circus and there was so much going on we couldn't take it all in? It was like that, Jenny, like a

three-ring circus. Now how about us getting serious about
the fence fixing? Want to ride in the pickup with me out to
the north range?"

"DON'T EXPECT TO RETURN TO NORMAL immediately. You
may have trouble sleeping."

Blake's mouth lifted in an ironic twist as he recalled the
doctor's words. He leaned against the frame of his bedroom window, moonlight splashing over his half-nude
body. He wore only his jeans as he stood looking out over
his ranch, his eyes growing used to the darkness, more
words from the doctor at the naval hospital echoing in his
ears. "We can't tell you what your emotional reaction to
being held captive will be. So much depends on the individual. In your case, you learned to distrust your captors
in order to survive. You may have to relearn to trust.

"But strangely enough, it will be yourself, your own
impressions and emotions you'll have the most difficulty
learning to accept. The people around you won't understand this. They'll interpret it as coldness and turn away
from you. You, in turn, will believe you were right to mis-
trust them in the first place.

"The best course is to realize you're going through a period of readjustment and give yourself some leeway. And
be patient. The human soul, like the body, does heal."

Blake could remember looking at the doctor and thinking how safe he must feel, giving a diagnosis hedged by
possibles, maybes and individual differences, neatly
capped by preaching tolerance. He didn't feel tolerant.
He'd been taken away from Jenny at the worst possible
time.

A curse on his breath, he tamped down the memories.
He wasn't—*wasn't*—going to hurt Jenny again the way he

had today. He was going to keep an iron hold on his
tongue . . . and his thoughts.

He stared down at the flat beauty of his ranch, the dark
shapes of the fences, the muted forms of the cattle graz-
ing. The night was almost as bright as day. An aching pride
filled him. This land, like Jenny, was his.

He frowned, remembering what his mother had told
him about the missing cattle. This land, like Jenny, had to
be guarded. It was a perfect night for rustlers, if they were
bold enough. Which they might be, thinking he would be
snug in bed on his first night home. Maybe he should give
them a little surprise.

That first little claw for fear curled deep inside him. And
for a moment he hated himself, hated his captors, hated
the fear they had taught him.

With a soft, low curse, he dressed, went to the barn,
saddled Storm, and with the rifle loaded and tucked under his arm, turned the horse out of the ranch lane. Once
they were on the straight moonlit road, he gave the stallion his head.

The landscape was flat and still, with a peculiar waiting quality, the shapes of trees with their tiny spring leaves
just rounded shadows on the plain. The sky was dark,
stabbed with stars, the moon brilliant. Splashed with silver, the night was beautiful. The cool, wine-clear air sliding over his cheeks poured elation over him. Best of all,
he was alone. There were no trucks, no man-shaped forms
stalking his cattle. No one.

He turned his face into the wind, absorbing the air like
a clay-dried empty vessel absorbs water. He was free.

There were no rotten ropes tying his hands, no empty
click of a pistol against his head. He could go anywhere
he cared to go, think any thought he cared to think. No,
he couldn't. The thought he'd been trying to suppress, the

thought that had brought him awake and driven him to ride into the chilly spring night still haunted him.

Had he lost his courage?

He continued to let Storm run free, knowing he'd pay for this ride with more than lost sleep. His softened thigh muscles would ache tomorrow. But he could no more stop riding into the soft, breeze-cooled night than he could stop breathing.

Blake rode until a pale streamer of peach silk shone along the bottom of the horizon. The sun glow broadened until there was a layer the color of a woman's skin next to the dark earth.

It was still too early for anyone to be up, but there were lights on in the house when he got back. A feather of fear touched him.

He urged Storm into a racing gallop, brought him up short in the yard and threw the reins over a post. When he opened the door, he saw his mother, her face drawn, and Jenny, clutching her waist, sobbing.

"What is it? What's wrong?"

Jenny looked up, made an incoherent sound of joy and ran for him. He opened his arms and scooped her sleep-warm body into them. "Jenny," he said huskily. "Jenny. It's all right."

"She woke up and went looking for you. I told her you had to be somewhere on the ranch, but she wouldn't believe me."

There was no reproach in his mother's voice, but it didn't matter. He felt guilty enough without it. He stroked the silk of Jenny's hair. "It's all right, honey. It's all right."

"I—thought—you—were gone again."

"I just took a ride—"

"You told me once it was dangerous to ride at night," Jenny said between sobs. "I went in your room, and I couldn't find you."

"Shh, babe. It's all right. How about coming out in the kitchen with me, and we'll see if we can find any of your grandma's good cinnamon rolls, shall we?"

Dark brown eyes lifted to his. "You won't leave me again, will you?"

"No, sweetheart. I won't leave you again."

MIDMORNING, in Jamie's apartment, the phone rang.

"The trap is set," Drew's voice drawled in her ear. Jamie lay in bed, fighting the need to close her eyes and go back to sleep, the phone receiver cradled between the pillow and her ear. A lazy golden sunshine filled the room, outlined the dust motes, spilled over the ruffled whiteness of her bed coverlet, telling her it was midmorning. "You aren't going to be able to escape the family dinner, after all. You've received a royal summons. You're to arise and prepare yourself for the festivities, and I'm to escort you there. A task which I find quite taxing but nevertheless salutary. I'm prepared to suffer all for the prodigal cousin."

Half asleep, wanting badly to laugh but loath to encourage him, Jamie threaded her slender fingers through her chestnut hair and wished she were a morning person. Words coming through a phone at ten o'clock on a Sunday didn't register clearly in her brain.

"Drew, I can't."

"I know, you have to wash your hair."

"As a matter of fact, I do."

"That's why I'm calling you two hours ahead of time."

"I really don't think—"

"My dear. You are laboring under the severe delusion that you have some choice in the matter. Believe me, pet, you don't. Prince Valiant just called and issued his decree, and he made it clear that his royal subjects were to do his bidding without delay."

"You're making that up."

"You know I wouldn't have the strength to concoct such a clever fiction so early in the morning."

"Blake wants me to come?"

An infinitesimal silence told her she shouldn't have asked him for verification. That one question betrayed too much. "Yes, he wants you to come." Drew's bored drawl was drier than it had been a moment ago. "That makes a difference, I take it?"

"Well, yes, I—"

"I wanted you to come yesterday."

"I know, but I—"

"You didn't want to do anything to encourage me." Another short, telling pause. "You wouldn't deny the long-suffering hero his fondest wish because of your aversion to him, would you?"

"I don't have an aversion to him," she said quickly, but Drew's short laugh told her he was not convinced.

"Don't try to lie to me, pet. You do it badly. Never mind about Blake. I want you to come, and I'm leveling the heavy artillery right now." In the quiet that followed, Jamie held her breath.

"Jenny had a bad night last night. She awoke and found Blake gone. To placate her, Blake promised he would ask you to come to dinner today. The child is sure you won't refuse, and she's quite ecstatic."

Jamie's first thought was for Jenny. How awful for the child to awake and find her father gone. Her next thought was that she had been very neatly blackmailed. Collecting herself, she said coolly, "I'm sure I don't know why your Viking ancestors ever went through all that bother of pillaging and plundering to get what they wanted. They could have just talked their way through the town, taking everything with their silver tongues and their innate flair for blackmail."

"Flattery will not avail you. I'll pick you up around eleven forty-five. Don't be late. Ruth expects to seat everyone at the first stroke of twelve, and woe to the unfortunate soul who forces her to wait."

"Drew—"

"I wasn't kidding about Jenny, Jamie." Drew's voice was cool, serious. "She had a scare last night, and Blake delivered you up as a diversion."

Jamie sighed and threw back the covers, thoroughly awake now, her plan to sleep until noon, prepare herself a leisurely brunch and spend the rest of the day doing whatever pleased her vanishing like smoke. "Those Viking ancestors of the two of you have a lot to answer for."

2

ARMOR. SHE NEEDED ARMOR. Something to make her look cool, sophisticated and poised. The exact opposite of what she felt.

Her gray suit would do it.

She found the suit and put it on, tucked a scarf in the neckline, made a face at herself in the mirror and stripped the length of silk away. She pulled a blouse from the closet, the blouse she hadn't wanted to wear, ignoring the nagging little voice in her mind that kept asking her just exactly who it was she was trying to impress. She'd spent most of the school year discouraging Drew.

Quiet, voice. Any actress knows you've got to look the part to play it. And there was Jenny. Her pupil would look at anything she wore with admiring eyes.

Eyes. Green eyes, hard emerald depths that gave no quarter. Jamie hadn't liked those eyes, but she couldn't forget them. No one could. They had looked too long and seen too much.

What had it been like to stand and watch the blade of that knife coming and know there was nothing you could do to stop it? She raised her hand to her cheek. Suppose it had been her flesh that had been scarred. How would she feel?

Proud. Defiant. Never letting her captors see her fear.

Who was she trying to kid? She'd be frightened out of her mind. Giving a half laugh at her heroic imaginings, and how far they were from reality, she finished dressing and carefully applied her makeup, her nerves singing. She had to stop thinking those thoughts. For if she didn't, Blake Lindstrom would take one look at her, know she had spent the morning pitying him and throw her out of the house.

When she had brushed her hair into shining submission, she slipped into gray suede high heels, three-inch ones that gave her five-foot-five height the edge she would need if she were to spend the afternoon fencing with the male portion of the Lindstrom clan.

She'd already crossed swords with Blake last fall, and she'd lost. Lindstrom was an expert at the art of verbal slice, cut and parry. She told herself she wasn't looking forward to seeing him again, but as she climbed into the car beside Drew, she was aware of a tingling in her body, a sense of aliveness. Whatever this visit to Blake Lindstrom's house might bring, it wouldn't be boredom.

Drew's glance flickered over the pale gray suit. He gave an approving whistle and started the car. "I like the blouse." His gaze lingered on the triangle of smooth skin above her breasts, exposed by the silk collar turned back over the suit lapels.

"Don't say it," she warned him.

He raised one golden eyebrow, feigning hurt dignity. "Don't say what? That I don't understand how you can look prim and proper and devastatingly sexy at the same time? Looking like that, you're going to have your hands full with my outspoken father. Thad will expect me to take you in hand—and offer for yours."

"And if I don't happen to love you—"

"He'll instruct me in the ungentle art of abducting you, zealously overseeing my efforts to throw you over my charger and carry you away."

"I'll have to give your father the news about the age of equality. A woman decides her own destiny these days."

Drew groaned. "Please, don't tell him that, or he'll turn that scatter-shot attack he normally reserves for Blake on you, and we'll be sitting at the table until nightfall with the two of you arguing."

"Is that why Blake insisted I come—to draw your father's fire away from him?"

Drew gave her a sidelong glance before he turned his face back to the road. "Why couldn't he have asked you for the obvious reason, that he wanted to see you?"

"He gave me the impression last fall that he'd be far happier if our paths never crossed again. And he seemed to feel the same way yesterday."

"I doubt if Blake feels the same about anything as he did six months ago."

"His attitude toward me is remarkably consistent."

Drew dropped one hand from the wheel, leaving the other to guide the car with the casual half attention the country road required. His classic profile was highlighted. "Aren't you being a little . . . sensitive about my cousin's reaction to you?"

"Am I?" She tried to achieve the same casualness. "I wasn't aware of it."

Drew continued to look out at the road. "It occurs to me, amateur psychiatrist that I am, that you're taking the easy way out."

"I don't know what you mean." But she did.

Nothing in Drew's face changed. He looked as smoothly handsome as ever. "If you feel that Blake doesn't like you, that gives you justification for not liking him. Don't get me wrong, sweet," he said quickly when she started to protest. "I'm all for a nice little spot of animosity between the two of you."

"I don't dislike Blake. I don't know him well enough to dislike him. He just makes me . . . uncomfortable. I can't help feeling sorry for him, but he obviously doesn't want my sympathy or anybody else's."

For a moment Drew's smooth mask dropped away, and some raw, primitive emotion shone from that hard face. "Don't feel sorry for Blake. He's impregnable. Nothing could hurt him."

"He loves his daughter."

"That may be his only redeeming feature."

"It almost makes up for all the rest. Men who are gentle with children are a rare breed. Maybe he takes after you. You're a natural with your students, Drew."

"There's nothing I like more than a captive audience."

"It's more than that, and you know it. You monitor those kids' progress very carefully."

Without moving a muscle Drew said, "It's a rough world out there. They need all they can get, and more, to survive. Sometimes it seems as if the world is just waiting to cut people up in little pieces. Look what happened to Blake—that is, if you can stand the sight."

"Don't," she said in a low voice, turning her head toward the countryside, bright in the spring sunshine and unmarred by scars.

"The worst of it is, it isn't the scar itself that repels you." Drew went relentlessly back to the topic of Blake. Her attempt to sidetrack him into talking about teaching hadn't worked at all. "It's the thought of how strong he must have been to survive such an ordeal. None of us have ever been called on to have that kind of strength...and probably we never will."

Drew's words uncannily echoed her own earlier thoughts. Was the sight of Blake's scar unnerving because it unearthed a deep-seated fear and sense of inadequacy in her?

Drew turned the car off the road. They pulled in under a beautifully cut sign, two *L*'s superimposed over each other, carved on dark wood and suspended on a thin wire from two tall posts.

Needing to think of something besides Blake's injury, Jamie asked, "Do the *L*'s stand for Blake and his father?"

Drew shook his head. "No, they represent my father and his. They ranched together until Blake's father died five years ago. Mine is the infamous Thad, whom you'll meet today. He lives in a house a few miles down the road. He retired unofficially two years ago, but he's been helping out during Blake's enforced vacation."

Blake Lindstrom's house was like him, full of texture and depth and surprises. Jenny met them at the door, hugged Jamie, said a shy hello to Drew and led them into the house. The central part was a great room, the old-fashioned concept of a room that was everything—living room, dining room and a place to keep warm by the fire. An old circular rag rug woven from soft-colored fabrics, in mulberry, cream and heliotrope, covered most of the wood floor. It was a rug that had been made with patience and love. Instinctively Jamie knew it had been Blake's mother who had sat and threaded the muted colors one over the other, not his wife.

A huge fireplace dominated one wall, the stones a rough granite that was strangely suited to the muted colors. There were other wonderfully creative touches, white button knobs on tiny oak lamp tables that matched the tiebacks on the drapes. The coffee table was a tree stump smoothed to a glossy finish. It held a primitive clay ashtray shaped like a child's hand, Jenny's, made in Betsy Bigelow's kindergarten class four years ago. Patchwork pillows, handcrafted by the same clever hand as the rug, softened the look of the well-worn, comfortable leather couch.

Blake stood leaning against the mantle, his scarred profile turned toward them. Jamie felt again the clenching of muscle at the sight of the marred flesh. She disciplined herself to maintain control of her face and gave him a smile, but his eyes told her she hadn't fooled him.

She'd been dreading this moment all morning, and he knew it.

And didn't care.

Everything about him told her that, the way he stood leaning against the fireplace with no emotion on his face, as if her entrance into his house was an event that hardly interested him.

Then why had he asked her to come? "Miss Gordon." The dark head bowed in her direction. "I'm so glad you were able to...adjust your schedule to be with us." His face might be a travesty of nature, but his voice almost made up for it. The quality was perfect, dark and deep like finely aged sherry, the tiny sting of irony preventing it from being too sexually inviting. Sexually inviting? That thought, coming on the heels of being not so gently chided about her reluctance to come, made color seep up her throat. She faced him, her chin high. "I was pleased to be asked."

Blake's face didn't change a particle. "It was our pleasure."

Something about his expression told her he knew his pleasantries were drawing blood. As if he was tiring of the game, his head swung in Drew's direction. "Cousin—" and remembering his duties as host "—what would you like to drink?"

"You know mine. Manhattan. Straight up. Jamie, what would you like?"

I'd like to leave. The words beat in her brain. She looked at Blake Lindstrom and, as if he knew exactly what she was thinking, a half smile tipped the corners of his mouth.

"We have white wine, which is, I believe, the traditional drink of maiden-lady schoolteachers."

She'd meant to ask for a glass of iced tea. Her blood warmed by anger, she forgot caution. "I'll have what Drew's having."

She'd gone insane. She loathed Manhattans. Intelligence, logic and reasoning—all had vanished simply because Blake had called her a maiden-lady schoolteacher.

"Sit down, please," Blake said smoothly. "Jenny can keep you company while I play bartender."

Jenny beamed, delighted to be entrusted with the responsibility Blake obviously didn't want. When Jamie moved around and sank into the leather couch, Jenny plopped beside her and began to chatter. Jamie heard herself making agreeing sounds, but for once in her life she wasn't giving the child her full attention. She couldn't. She was too painfully conscious of Blake watching her for that minute second before he turned and left the room, a look in his eyes that was totally indecipherable.

On his return, it was worse. He deftly handed her the drink without touching her, but as he went back to take his place next to the mantle, she was more conscious of him than ever.

You are being ridiculous, her mind mocked her as she sipped the drink she didn't want and tried to look as if she liked it. *This will gain you nothing. Blake Lindstrom does not like you, and nothing you can say or do will change his mind.*

Why on earth would you want to change his mind?

She was relieved when Jenny began to talk about the project Jamie had assigned to the class. Everybody was to read a fairy tale, then create a scene in clay from the story. Not a very original idea, Jamie knew, but the principal had insisted that each class have a project ready for the end-of-the-year exposition he planned to hold during the last week of school.

"You encourage your pupils to read fairy tales?"

It was the first time Blake had directed his words at Jamie since he'd greeted her, and his faintly disapproving tone put her teeth on edge. "Yes," she said, clutching her drink in a nervous effort to keep from spilling it, hoping her clipped answer would stop him from pursuing the topic. He would be the last person in the world to believe in, or approve of, the reading of fairy tales; she knew that.

"Why not concentrate on a piece of nonfiction? A travelogue, perhaps, or an account of a historic event?"

She had long ago made it a rule never to discuss her beliefs about the work she assigned her children as if the children themselves were not there. "Perhaps if you're really interested, we could discuss it some other time." Jamie sipped her drink and hoped she looked as cool as her voice sounded.

"Jenny, run to the kitchen for a moment and see if your grandmother needs any help."

Jenny looked at her father in distress, obviously torn between wanting to please him and staying with Jamie.

"You can sit by Miss Gordon at the table. Now, go, sweet."

Heaving a sigh, Jenny got to her feet. "All right, Daddy." Her back to him, she mumbled, "Why didn't you just say you wanted me to leave the room?"

When she had gone through the swinging doors at the other end of the room, Blake allowed a brief smile to lift his lips. "That child seems to have gotten precocious in the past six months."

"Maybe she's been forced to," Jamie replied.

"Maybe she has. Maybe she's been forced to accept reality. A lesson that seems to come to all of us . . . which makes me wonder why valuable school time should be used studying fantasy."

She shot a quick, irritated glance at Drew, saw his lazy, comfortable sprawl and the half smile on his lips and knew there would be no help from him. Taking a tighter grip on her glass, she waded into the fray. "Nonfiction doesn't appeal to preadolescents the way fantasy does. I'm trying to encourage the children to use their natural flair for creative imagination before they get older and lose it."

"Would you have them divorce themselves from reality?"

"No, of course not," she shot back. "Nor will they because of this one assignment. They deal with reality every day, just as we all do—" She stopped, knowing she had said too much and wishing she could retract it all.

Drew lifted his glass and said, "Hear, hear." She shot him an angry look. He'd be lucky if she didn't toss this favorite drink of his in his face.

Where the conversation would have gone after that, she'd never know. Blake's mother came in, said hello to Jamie and Drew and told them she was ready for them to be seated at the table.

The dining part of the room was delineated by another oval multicolored rug and an oval pine table. The dishes were a deep delft blue, the glasses a lighter, clearer blue. The chair cushions were a glowing velvet mulberry. Everything looked lovely and homey and welcoming, except the expression on the face of the man who was going to sit directly across from Jamie.

His mocking gaze didn't keep her from noticing how slowly and carefully he lowered himself into his chair. His mother noticed it, too. "Blake? What's the matter? Have you hurt yourself?"

A dark look of impatience flashed across his face. "A few pulled muscles. Nothing a hot bath won't cure."

He'd been riding, Jamie thought suddenly, and he wasn't in shape for it. Another price he'd been forced to pay because of his captivity. He glanced up, saw her look of concern, and the momentary softening of his face vanished. His features turned to tempered steel.

Thad came storming in, throwing an apologetic look at Ruth, blustering about the poor condition of the roads and casting a shrewd, assessing look in Jamie's direction as Drew introduced her.

The first part of the meal was easy enough. The men talked, much of their conversation centering on the ranch work. Jenny wasn't eating a lot, Jamie saw, but that wasn't unusual for her. The child had a small appetite.

The food was delicious—traditional Western steak done to a turn, mashed potatoes, green salad and winter squash baked with brown sugar. Jamie tried to do justice to the food, but she was too aware of Blake. What was he thinking as he lounged in that comfortable chair across from her, eating almost as little as Jenny?

But toward the end of the meal, curious crosscurrents began to flow. To Jamie, two things were obvious. Drew's father cared for Ruth...and he wished that Blake were his son. It was an eerie thing to watch Thad Lindstrom look at Ruth with hunger in his eyes. It was even stranger to see that look turned on Blake. There was admiration for the younger man gleaming out from under those heavy gray brows.

Jamie dropped her eyes, feeling as if she'd eavesdropped or peeped into a forbidden room. For the first time she began to understand Drew's curious relationship with Blake.

Blake seemed immune to his uncle's regard. He gave Thad the same polite attention he gave everyone. But the uneasiness, the feeling that she was waiting for something to happen, would not leave her.

Her instincts were right. At the end of the meal, Blake leaned forward in his chair and gave her a straight, uncompromising look. "Drew tells me you're a competent rodeo performer. Would you like to come out to the stable and see my Arabian stallion?"

Did she want to see a beautiful horse? That was like asking a chocolate addict to take a tour through a candy factory. Of course she wanted to see the horse.

But do you want to be alone with this man?

He couldn't be as clairvoyant as he seemed to be. He couldn't read her mind. But as he sat there waiting for her decision, he seemed to. As if he were certain she would refuse, he relaxed back in his chair, his eyes never leaving her face.

"I'd like that very much. How kind of you to ask." She rose from the table, feeling like a Christian emerging victorious from a pride of lions.

"Mother, if you'll excuse us? Uncle?" Blake surprised his uncle from some pattern of deep thought. He'd been sitting there scowling, his reverie set off by Blake's invitation to see his horse, it seemed to Jamie. "What? Oh, not at all, my boy, not at all."

Jamie had taken her jacket off before dinner and tossed it over the back of the sofa. As she walked toward it, Blake followed her to the couch and plucked it up before she could reach it.

He held the garment, his lean fingers lost in the soft gray wool. "Will you manage all right in those shoes?" His eyes traveled down her sleek legs to the suede pumps she wore, his face cool with polite concern.

"I'll be careful."

He helped her slip into the jacket, murmuring something she couldn't hear. When he reached up to adjust the collar and his fingers brushed her bare neck, she tensed.

"I'm sorry," he said softly. "Did I hurt you?"

So polite. So mocking.

"No. No, of course not."

The spring air was cool, and as she stepped out into the yard, she shivered. Without any overt move that she could see, Blake was beside her, his body shielding hers from the wind. "Instead of worrying about your ankles, I should have gotten a coat for you."

She could feel the heat of his body, the rub of his jacket. "I'm all right." She wasn't, but not for the world would she have admitted it to this man who strode along beside her. In spite of the stiffness he had admitted to, he moved with an easy grace that was as magnetic to the eye as it was disturbing to the senses.

Inside the stable, the proud, black horse in the first stall tossed his mane and whickered a warning. The velvety nostrils quivered with anticipation; the head was thrown back with pride. He was a glorious specimen of horseflesh, and he knew it.

Jamie carefully picked her way down the straw-covered aisle on her teetering heels, one hand moving along the top of the stall wall to help her keep her balance, heading for the horse like a bee to a flower.

"Watch it. Storm doesn't tolerate strangers."

"I'm not a stranger. Not to him." Jamie stood outside Storm's stall, offering her hand to the animal to sniff with the respect and obvious deference of a subject seeking audience with a king.

Blake stared. The sight of his great brute of a stallion nuzzling this strange woman's hand and emitting a throaty croon gave him the distinct feeling that his eyes were lying to him. "I should have known. What are you doing to him?"

"Just talking."

The glossy chestnut head of the woman bent closer to the blue-black muzzle of the horse. She hadn't cut her hair stylishly short. It grew long and natural, curling on the ends. The sheen of it as it fell over her shoulders made him want to pick it up and let it slide through his fingers, to see if it was as silky as it looked....

She began to make sounds that were a feminine version of Storm's, a low, throaty croon that was as much a pleasure to Blake's ears as the sight of her was to his eyes.

"What are you telling him?"

She looked up at him, and for a moment he could have sworn she'd forgotten he was there. Her concentration on the horse was total. "I'm telling him what he already knows—that he's a beautiful, strong male."

Blake folded his arms and leaned against the stall, his eyes dark in the shadowed barn. "Beauty, as they say, is in the eyes of the beholder." He waited, watching those dark blue eyes of hers play over his face.

A long, quiet moment followed, and then she lifted her head, as if she'd made a decision. "There is a story about a man and a mask," she said slowly. "Do you know it?"

"I don't have your repertoire of fairy tales."

She ignored the slight gibe. "The man in the story has a face that is terribly...disfigured. He has a mask made, one that gives him the appearance of a gentle, loving man."

"And?"

"He begins to take on the characteristics of a gentle, loving man to match the mask. When he takes it off many years later, he discovers a miracle has taken place. His own face looks exactly like the mask. He had become the good and gentle man that the mask portrayed."

"I'm sure this story must apply to me, but I don't see how."

"Your case is just the opposite. You mustn't let your mind become as . . . distorted as your mask." Her blood beat wildly in her veins; her nerves danced.

He didn't move. For what seemed like an eternity, he stood there, his eyes locked with hers. "How do you know I haven't already done that, Ms. Gordon?"

The mockery was at its summit, cool, cutting. "I wasn't suggesting . . ."

Slowly, deliberately, he unfolded his arms and laid them along the top of the stall, exposing his entire body to her gaze. "Stop idealizing me."

"I'm not idealizing you—"

"Then stop gazing at me with those gorgeous eyes full of the sympathy and the most delightful come-on I've had in ages—" he straightened away from the stall "—or I'll be tempted to prove just how far from being the idealistic hero of your dreams I really am."

Her face hot with embarrassment and fury, she said, "I haven't been coming on to you."

"No?" He took a step closer.

Her eyes flashing, she said, "The only thing I feel for you is the same thing any other person might feel—human compassion."

He stood where he was, his face like stone. "I don't want your human compassion."

"Well, it's a darn good thing, because it just went into short supply."

"I wonder." He took a step closer. "Even if you tried, I wonder if you could stop putting me up on that pedestal of yours."

As Blake watched, Jamie stepped back and turned toward Storm, her hand cupping his jaw. She had long fingers, graceful but strong, a sure sign that she rode often and well. Only her profile was visible, but he could see how finely made her bones were, how silky her skin was. She was beautiful. A beautiful young woman. And one he had to discourage.

"If I did put you on a pedestal, you're fast falling off it," she said in a low, furious tone.

He stepped forward again, and every muscle in Jamie's body tightened. She didn't move. She couldn't. He took the last step that brought him to her and grasped her shoulders with his hands. "And not a moment too soon." He stood in front of her like a shadow blocking the aisle, cutting off any attempt she might have made to walk away. "I'm a man, not a statue. I have a man's taste and a man's curiosity. . . ."

Carefully, as if he were touching glass, he reached for a strand of chestnut hair lying over her shoulder and pulled it forward, smoothing it down over her collarbone.

Fire ignited under her jacket where his fingers touched her, turning her skin to flame.

His face changed subtly, as if he sensed her reaction to his touch. She met his gaze, determined not to betray the riotous state of her senses. By the force of her will alone she stood there, waiting for whatever he would do next.

"I was right," he said. "Your hair feels like the sun, just as I thought it would. And so do you. You could warm the coldest man's soul in the world with that sweet smile of yours." He moved again, only a step, and yet she was trapped between him and the stall, and his hands were sliding up her back with a warmth and possession that had her reeling. "And how would it feel to taste your sweet warm breath in my mouth and hold your bare, smooth body in my arms? What are you like when you make love to a man, Jamie? Are you slow, sweet and shy... as if it were always the first time... or hot, passionate and desperate, as if it were always the last?"

The wine-dark voice was intoxicating. Dangerous, far too dangerous to stay in his arms... but impossible to leave. He was close enough that his face loomed in front of her in all its marred beauty.

He leaned forward and brushed her lips with his. She didn't flinch away. His mouth was foreign to her, warm and firm, the corner closest to his scarring pulled with tension. Alien. Unlike any male mouth she'd ever kissed. Frightening. Fascinating. And gone before she could fully taste its sweetness. "We're on a collision course," he murmured, his breath warm on her skin. "Your idealism against my realism." He nibbled along her cheek. "I wonder if we could find a common ground." He kissed her eyelid. "Perhaps if we searched long enough, some area of... mutual interest might occur to us."

She opened her mouth to protest, and he swooped to capture her lips with his, letting her learn the delights of being held by a man who knew what a woman needed. She'd been kissed before, but not like this. He made subtle discoveries, learned how she retreated, then, shyly, advanced. There was delight in his mouth, and humor and restraint. He made it easy to respond—suddenly the restraint vanished; in its place a heated hunger flowed from his body to hers, or hers to his—she wasn't sure which.

He made a low sound of satisfaction and took control like a conquering victor, one hand moving down the small of her back to lift her away from the stall and press her hips against his, the other circling her shoulders and holding her to receive the rhythmic possession of his kiss.

Desire, with a strength she never guessed it could have, spiraled upward, pushing aside common sense and reason. She'd never wanted a man like this before, a man she barely knew and wasn't sure she liked.

She felt the hard boards of the stall pressing against her back as Blake leaned into her, and then there was nothing. The warmth of his hands and his mouth were gone. He moved away from her, back into the shadows. "Stay away from me, sweet idealist. Or I might forget I don't want to take a woman to bed who sees me as a figure in a fairy tale."

TIKI'S HAT, bright and saucy like the woman herself, hung on the door of Jamie's apartment, welcoming Jamie home. "Good grief," Tiki had said one day early last fall, "this apartment is positively dismal." And characteristically, she had returned on her next visit with a straw hat decorated with bright red ribbons and dried flowers. "Use it as a door decoration. That way you'll feel good about coming in the place for a few minutes at least."

Inside her apartment, Jamie kicked off her high-heeled shoes and shrugged out of her suit jacket, keeping her turmoil at bay.

I won't think about it yet. Not yet. She padded around the apartment in her stocking feet, wishing she felt hungry enough to eat. She didn't. Later on in the day, Mrs. Lindstrom had insisted on serving a "light snack," which consisted of everything they'd had for dinner plus a plate of cold cuts, cheese and fluffy homemade buns. Jamie didn't think she'd need to eat again for a week. The worst part had been sitting across from Blake Lindstrom and trying to act normal. And trying to hide the fact that she was acting.

On the way home, she had learned just how unsuccessful she'd been.

"I detected some undercurrents at the luncheon table," Drew said. "Blake wasn't easing his trauma by making a pass at you out in the barn, was he?"

"You know, it's strange. I keep having this eerie feeling about the two of you. You make me feel as if I'm looking at the positive and the negative of a picture."

"Does that mean you're not going to answer my question?"

She smiled. "That's exactly what it means."

"Don't get mixed up with him, my pet. He's ruthless and heartless."

"And related to you."

"I know him better than you do, Jamie. The man has no heart."

"It's too bad, really," she said as if thinking out loud. "Under other circumstances, you might have been the best of friends."

"I've noticed that streak of idealism in you from time to time. I'm sure my cousin won't hesitate to capitalize on it."

They stopped in front of the big house that contained her apartment. Drew shut off the engine of the car and leaned back in the seat. It was sunset, a pale peach sky, and Jamie looked out across the landscape and felt as if she'd been riding a windmill all day. Why were all the males around her harping on her idealism? She wasn't idealistic. She was practical, logical and too smart to get involved with either of these predatory Vikings.

"You look as if you've had your fill of Lindstrom men."

Perceptive. Drew was bright and perceptive, and he shared her ideas about teaching. Why couldn't she care for him? "Now that you mention it, I think I have."

"Which probably means it would be a waste of my breath to ask you to have dinner with me next Friday."

"Drew, please."

His eyes gleamed. "Wouldn't I like to hear you say those words to me under different circumstances."

"I wonder if you really would." Leaving him with that bit of honesty to think about, she'd gotten out of the car.

The afternoon was over. She hadn't won, but she'd survived. She sank into the supersoft pillows of the couch, stretched out a stocking foot in the darkened apartment.

She thought about what had happened in the stable . . . and unbelievably, her mouth began to tingle in physical reaction to the memory of Blake's kiss.

This was madness. She didn't like him. Worse, he obviously didn't like her.

Then why had he kissed her? And why had she allowed it?

She lay back on the sofa, stretching lazily like a cat. There was a sensual awareness beating through her veins, a residual memory of the way he'd kissed her and made her feel. There had been other men in her life who'd kissed her with passion, but never one she'd wanted nearly as much. . . .

She was being foolish. It was a nonproblem. She would see him again, but at least not alone. Her world revolved around school and her friends and her riding. It would be easy, very easy to put Blake Lindstrom out of her life. She would probably never see or talk to him again, unless they were at a school or community function. She put her head back, and into her safe, quiet world, the world Blake Lindstrom would never be a part of, the phone rang.

She padded into her kitchen to answer it, her heart thumping in her chest. "Hello?"

"I'm calling to apologize."

There was an intimacy in the way Blake neglected to identify himself, as if he expected her to recognize his voice instantly. Which she did. "Why do you feel you need to do that?"

There was a pause. He didn't know how to deal with her bluntness. "I didn't have a chance to speak to you alone before you left. I want your assurance that you won't allow what happened between us to affect your attitude toward Jenny."

Shock made her go rigid. "You do believe in adding insult to injury, don't you?"

Another silence. Could he hear her breathing quicken? She was furious, her hand clenching at her side. All her fine resolutions to consign Lindstrom to the outer limits of her life went flying. She'd like to strangle him. He was lucky he was on the other end of the phone.

"That . . . wasn't my intention."

Through gritted teeth she said, "I think that was exactly your intention. You wanted to prove to me very clearly that you see me as an emotional female without a scrap of integrity. Well, believe me, you've made your point."

"I was worried about Jenny," he said gruffly.

"Nothing you do or say will have the slightest effect on the way I treat her."

"I'm glad to hear it—"

She allowed herself the small satisfaction of putting the phone down, hoping the click sounded very loud in his ear—and very final.

BLAKE STOOD IN HIS BEDROOM in the dark and undid the buttons on his shirt one by one. He would force himself to accept the dark, to know it again as a friend and not an enemy. In the dark, he would think logical thoughts about Jamie Gordon. He would recognize the truth, that he'd bungled quite badly.

He'd invited her out to the stable because he'd wanted to tell her to stay away, that he wasn't interested in her sympathy or the invitation that lay in those dark blue eyes. Did she believe he meant it? Probably not. He'd been compelled by a raging desire he hadn't felt in years to touch her, kiss her, and she seemed to have felt the same need....

He recalled her tone of voice on the phone and cursed under his breath. She had a right to be furious with him. He wasn't too happy with himself.

Stripped to his shorts, he lay down on his bed, pulled up the covers and stared at the ceiling.

He was physically attracted to Jamie Gordon, that was all, and she, with her idealistic fantasies, had developed a certain ... fascination for him. He'd meant to discourage her, and instead he'd ended up kissing her. Her body had been pliant, yielding in his arms. He wanted to hold her again and feel her mouth open under his, responsive, taking and giving....

He stared into the darkness, knowing it was going to be another long night.

3

MONDAY MORNING, Jamie clipped along on the sidewalk, heading for school and carrying on a brisk mental dialogue with herself.

For heaven's sake, act naturally when you see Jenny.

Of course I'll act naturally. There's no reason I shouldn't.

There's one big reason, one six-foot-three-inch-tall reason.

Forget him. He may be Jenny's father, but he has nothing to do with your relationship with her.

Jamie reached the school and stepped into her classroom. As the halls began to resound with noise and the children came in off the school buses, she discovered her apprehensions were unnecessary. Jenny was absent from school.

In the afternoon, feeling that she'd been carrying the weight of the world on her shoulders and it had fallen off at last, she went to the faculty room to take her break and drink a cup of coffee.

Teachers went there in a state of exhaustion to escape the noise and energy level in the building; they cared little about their surroundings. If anyone had decorated the room, it had been someone other than a faculty member. The school secretary had supplied a potted plant and saw to it that it was watered. If she didn't, it would have expired in three days. A rotating slate of two teachers, dubbed the Dynamic Duo, was responsible for washing stray cups and picking up old newspapers. The table groaned under the weight of newsprint because, it seemed, this week's current duo was more lethargic than dynamic.

The room had more character than the one at the last school where Jamie had taught. There were similarities: the coffee urn at the counter beside the sink, a long table with straight-back chairs, a broken-down couch backed against the wall as if taking its last stand. But the Rock Falls faculty room was different from all others because of the signs.

One Halloween two years ago, a prankster with imagination had tried to brighten the atmosphere by attaching exotic labels to everything, a double newspeak effort. On the inside of the door hung the sign, Den of Iniquity. The urn from which Jamie was drawing a cup of coffee had been designated the Oasis. The bulletin board behind the urn sported the heading, Newport Daily News.

On the board below the sign hung the principal's current message about the weekly teachers' meeting. Beside it was a missive in block printing from Betsy Bigelow, the kindergarten teacher, asking for volunteers to work on the cleanup crew for the Parent Teacher carnival on May 10. Below that, secured by a green thumbtack, was a picture of Blake and an article about him.

Arrested in the act of sipping her coffee, Jamie supported one slender arm with the other cupped round her elbow. She stared at the picture. It was nothing but a crude image in black ink dots on white paper. Yet even with his face half turned from the camera, the compelling power of the man was there. The night before last, she'd been exposed to the real thing, to the heat and depth and attraction of Blake Lindstrom.

Ridiculous. The whole idea, the whole thought of her being attracted to Blake was ridiculous. She was not attracted to him. She disliked him intensely. And the feeling was mutual.

Jamie twisted away from the board and walked around the table where the teachers ate their noon meals, the Feeding Trough, to sink into the Love Boat, the sway-backed relic couch from a former principal's family room that he'd been unkind enough to leave behind when he'd moved on. The chair where the present principal, Tom Coachman, sat sported the title, Coachman's In.

The teachers had voted unanimously to leave the signs. They were a tribute in their own way and proved, if nothing else, that one adolescent's imagination had been stirred.

Jamie relaxed back and thought about the meeting they'd had a week ago Monday night. The Rock Falls school was typical of most schools in rural South Dakota: it was small. The top floor of the old brick building housed the high school and junior high students, and the grade-school rooms were on the bottom floor. The total enrollment averaged about three hundred pupils, approximately twenty-five per class.

There had been attempts by a larger school district to the north to absorb Rock Falls, none of which had been successful...yet. But those in favor of consolidation were on the move again. And if they were successful, the school would be closed. The faculty would have to find jobs elsewhere, an idea that did not appeal to Jamie. She'd only come to Rock Falls last fall, and she didn't want to have it on her record that she'd moved two years in a row. And there was her rodeo riding. Rock Falls was an excellent location for her to board Strawberry close by and train both the mare and herself.

Jamie sipped her coffee absently. Money was the issue, of course. The people in the Rock Falls District wanted their school to continue. But Winchester, the school to the north, needed more money. And a sure way to get more money was to take in more territory and enlarge enrollment.

The door whacked to the wall, and Teresa Karolyn Jones stormed into the room. Tiki was only five feet two inches tall, but she had hair the color of flame and a personality to match. She taught seventh- and eight-grade homeroom subjects with a wizardry that constantly amazed Jamie, and she kept twenty-eight junior high boys and girls and their runaway hormones under control.

Tough love. Tiki seemed to have invented the phenomenon. Her kids would have walked through fire for her if she'd asked them to.

"The next time I decide to include a course in creative writing in my English class, take me immediately to the nearest shrink and have my head examined."

"Trouble?" Jamie asked, raising a dark brow and wondering why Tiki could make a room brighter just by being in it. Tiki plopped on the couch beside her, forcing Jamie to grab her cup to keep from spilling coffee all over her lap. "You have exactly ten minutes to tell me about it, Tiki."

"I was trying to teach the kids about creating character. We were working on a hero together as a class activity to get their brains going. They'd already decided their hero should be a race-car driver. I, in my infinite wisdom, explained that even though he was a hero, he should have a handicap, some kind of a scar, perhaps one he'd picked up in an accident on the track. John Wheeling said he wouldn't have accidents—he was too good a driver. Carol Hennings suggested the accident could have been another driver's fault. We were going back and forth like that and getting exactly nowhere when Tom Carconne came up with what he assured us would be a super handicap. 'Let's make him impotent,' my most brilliant of students said."

Jamie chuckled. "What did you say to that?"

"I didn't have to say anything. My innocent, Carol—you know, the one whose father took their TV set out and heaved it on the junk pile when she was seven? She turns to Tom and says, 'What does that mean?' There I am turning thirty shades of purple, when all Tom does is grin at her and say in that wiseacre voice of his, 'It means he has two broken legs.'" Tiki rolled her eyes to the ceiling, and Jamie laughed.

"What did you say?"

"Well, I broke every axiom my creative writing teacher taught me, clamped down on their creativity and made a decision for them. I said I'd seen those race-car drivers on TV, and they rarely broke one leg, let alone two, and I thought our driver ought to have a facial scar—that would be more believable. Of course, Tom knew what I was up to. Aren't you drinking cream in your coffee?"

Tiki's ability to both observe and feed data through her lightning-keen mind was one of the reasons she got along well with her equally volatile charges. Jamie thought her friend's sharpness might well be her own undoing.

"I decided I needed my caffeine straight this morning."

"Lord, here it is Tuesday already and you're still feeling the effects of your weekend? I thought you were going to call me when you got home from Ye Olde Lindstrom Homeplace."

"I was going to but I'm afraid I . . . forgot."

"I see. You must have had an interesting day." Tiki left the couch and walked around the table to draw a cup of coffee. She stood by the bulletin board, sipping it thoughtfully, her eyes on the picture. Then she turned back to Jamie. With a face as innocently sober as an earnest child's, she said, "I'd bet my last dollar that man doesn't have two broken legs."

Jamie nearly dumped her coffee in her lap. "Tiki, for heaven's sake."

Looking undaunted, Tiki moved to the sofa and sat down on the arm. "I wonder if somebody shut me up for six months if I'd come out looking like that—lean and controlled and dangerous, like a panther on the prowl."

The door to the faculty room opened. "My dear," Drew drawled as he came into the room, "nobody could shut you up for six seconds, let alone six months."

Tiki picked up a pillow and pitched it at Drew. He fended off the blow with poise. Like every woman with eyes in her head, Tiki adored Drew, but he treated her to the same cool courtesy and needling words that he did everyone. She loathed his self-control and kept trying to chip away at it. So far she hadn't been successful in perturbing him even slightly. "You're just jealous because everybody's talking about your cousin."

"If it were possible for me to be jealous of my cousin, little one, I'd have arrived at the pinnacle of that undesirable state long ago." His smooth, broad back, clad in a neat broadcloth shirt in the palest shade of blue, turned to them. Jamie steadied her coffee, gave Tiki a sharp elbow in the ribs and shook her head warningly. Tiki's response was predictable.

In a voice loud enough for everyone in the room to hear, she said to Jamie, "What's wrong? What have I done?"

Drew turned from the coffee urn and looked at them across the top of the newspaper-strewn table, his eyes meeting Jamie's. His dark glance swung to Tiki. "Don't disturb yourself. You haven't done a thing. Jamie sometimes forgets I'm not one of her third graders."

"I should think it would be Jamie who needs protection from you."

"She has her own defenses. And very effective ones, too."

There was a sudden and complete silence. Jamie felt Tiki's stillness.

Elaborately casual, the red-haired woman said, "Does that mean you've already tried to breach them?"

"That's hardly any of your business, is it?"

Jamie stood up, went to the sink and sloshed out her cup. "I'd love to stay and listen to this conversation about me, but my troops are due. Try not to cause a scandal while I'm gone, will you?"

She managed to get out of the room before Tiki's thrown pillow connected with her back.

The rest of the day was equally unproductive, and while the thought of Tiki and Drew nagged at the back of her mind, she wasn't allowed the luxury of thinking about them. Twenty-two third graders had a way of commanding attention. Billy Clauson bloodied his nose on the merry-go-round, Jennifer's dress got caught on the jungle gym and the entire hem tore out and Tim Morris spent his free reading time watching the gerbil and asking in a plaintive voice why Henry wasn't going to have babies.

AT NINE O'CLOCK, Tiki, dressed in her robe and floppy slippers, was sitting in Jamie's tiny living room cross-legged in front of the TV set, plucking popcorn out of the bowl resting precariously on one knee. She'd brought her things for overnight. Rather than go back to the trailer house she rented on the other side of town, she was staying with Jamie for the evening. Jamie was pleased to have her stay but not pleased with the topic of conversation.

Tiki had somehow, during the course of their talk about the day at school, found out that Jenny was absent.

"Why are you so worried about her?"

"She seemed perfectly all right yesterday when I was with her."

"That doesn't mean anything. You know how fast kids can get sick."

The thought that had been haunting her all day came back in full force. Had Blake kept Jenny away from school on purpose?

"You still haven't told me how your day went with the Lindstroms. Did Blake talk about his captivity?"

"No. No one asked, and he didn't volunteer anything."

"Sounds like he's being as closemouthed about it with his family as he was with the press. I wonder if he's told anybody what it was like."

"Maybe there wasn't anything to tell. Most of the rest of them said they were well treated and that nothing happened except that one incident with the women, when Blake took on that mercenary."

"Proving he had more guts than sense."

"He did manage to protect the women."

"Yes, but at the expense of his face. That's a pretty high price to pay. Sir Walter Raleigh only lost his cloak." Tiki hitched her robe up and eyed the television set they'd been watching with casual lack of interest. "Did you talk to him at all Sunday?"

"Yes, I talked to him."

"What did you talk about?"

"Imagination and reality."

"You would. Good grief, Jamie, didn't anyone ever teach you how to flirt?"

Jamie turned to look at Tiki, her face bland. "Why should I flirt with Blake Lindstrom?"

Tiki's freckled face colored. "Because he's available and so are you."

"An excellent premise for a lasting relationship," Jamie said dryly.

"All right, all right, I admit it. So I'd like you tangled up with some other male to leave me a field clear with Drew. Actually, I don't think it would make any difference if you dropped off the edge of the earth. He still wouldn't look at me."

"I don't think he's your type, Tiki. Really. You need someone more open."

"And less infatuated with you."

"Drew isn't—"

Tiki shook her head. "Let's not go over that old ground. So tell me. Did you and the master philosopher Blake come to any conclusions about imagination and reality, life and death?"

"We agreed to disagree."

"I barely know what that means, so I'm certainly not going to ask what you talked about. What is he really like, Jamie?" Tiki stretched her shoulders, rolled her eyes and popped a piece of popcorn in her mouth.

"You think after one evening spent with him I know? The man is tremendously . . . self-contained. I have a feeling he was that way before he went through this current thing, and it has made him even more so." Jamie lay back on the couch as if she weren't really interested in their topic of conversation.

Tiki stared at the television set and frowned, holding a piece of popcorn in midair. "Certainly doesn't sound like the type who would volunteer to man the kissing booth at the parent-teacher fair, does he?"

Jamie came upright. *"What?"*

Tiki went on gazing at the TV, ignoring the effect her words had on Jamie. "Funny. You wouldn't think shy little Betsy would have had the nerve to ask him, would you? Maybe he likes the shy type. That probably means I'm out of the running, huh?" She peered up at Jamie, a grin lifting her generous mouth.

"Are you sure?"

"That I'm not the shy type or that Betsy asked him? Actually, I'm sure of both things. Betsy said she'd asked him to help and he'd agreed, and then I asked her what he was going to do, and she said he was going to be in the kissing booth. Does my story hold together, counselor?"

"Wait a minute. You say Betsy asked him to help and told you he was going to be in the kissing booth? Did she tell *him* that?"

"Well, I assume so."

"Never assume anything with Betsy."

Tiki frowned in mock severity. "I wasn't aware she had a problem."

"She thinks everybody is in her kindergarten class and they all understand her without her having to explain anything." Jamie sank back on the couch, her hand on her forehead. "Do you think she told him what she wanted him to do?"

"Your guess is as good as mine." Tiki slanted a look up at Jamie. "Maybe somebody should make certain."

"I suppose somebody should. But who? Not Betsy, surely."

"You're the one who got invited to the family dinner," Tiki said slyly, popping another piece of the buttery corn into her mouth and turning her hand to point an accusing finger at Jamie.

"Didn't they tell you in teachers' college not to point your finger at people? You make me feel as if I'm looking at an old World War II poster. Uncle Sam wants *you*."

"And you're the one who went to the barn with him."

"It's lucky for you I'm not the violent type, Miss Jones."

"Argh!" Tiki folded her arm under her and rolled over on top of a pillow, scattering the popcorn in several directions. "Don't call me that, please. Uncle, uncle."

"That's why your kids love you so much. You're such easy prey."

"And your kids love you so much because you're so fey. Horses, children, men—they're all putty in your hands. You're just the woman to take on Blake Lindstrom."

Jamie picked up a pillow and made an earnest effort to cover Tiki's face with it.

But later, lying in bed, listening to Tiki's slow, even breathing, she knew her friend was right. She was the only one to take on the task of discovering if Blake Lindstrom knew exactly what he'd volunteered for.

THE NEXT DAY, on the playground during noon hour, with the shouts of children at a distance making conversation just barely possible between the two watching teachers, Jamie caught Betsy's arm. "How is the fair coming?"

Looking not much older than her charges, Betsy Bigelow turned a face rosy with wind kisses up to Jamie and smiled at her. "Absolutely fabulous. I have all the booths manned and full rosters for the kitchen and cleanup crews. Why? Have you decided you'd rather not be the candy girl, after all?"

"No, there's no problem there. I just wondered—who did you get to do the kissing booth?"

"Blake Lindstrom," Betsy said promptly.

The cool spring wind bit at Jamie's cheeks. "Does he understand what he's volunteering for?"

"Of course he does. And anyway, it wouldn't matter. He said he'd be glad to do anything I thought he was capable of doing."

"Wait a minute. Did you mention the kissing booth specifically?"

"Of course I did. When I called, I told him what vacancies I had left—the kissing booth, the ring toss and the duck pond—and he said he'd be glad to help wherever I needed him."

"Betsy, he may have thought you wouldn't consider him for the kissing booth because that's usually done by a woman."

"But just think of all the women in the community who will want to kiss Blake."

Jamie wondered how many there were. If only Betsy didn't float around in the upper stratosphere. "But does Blake want to kiss them?"

Betsy looked at her blankly. "Why would he object to being kissed?"

On that note of logic, Jamie conceded defeat and retired from the field.

She spent the rest of the week considering various plans of action and discarding them, one after another, as distinctly unsuitable. A note home with Jenny was not the answer and had the added disadvantage of being open to misinterpretation. A request to Drew to talk to his cousin was equally unworkable.

On Wednesday morning, the problem of the kissing booth was driven from her mind by one more serious. Jenny still hadn't returned to school.

Jamie's phone call to Mrs. Lindstrom left her feeling even more disturbed.

"She had a stomach ailment. We're not sure what it is. The doctor is coming out again tomorrow."

Thursday and Friday dragged by with equal parts of boredom and child-generated crises of various kinds. Tim finally succeeded in letting the gerbil out of its cage when Jamie wasn't looking, and Jennifer's mother had called to say that she wasn't happy about her daughter's dress being torn. As the crowning touch, Jamie was behind on the attendance reports that were due at the end of the month.

The thought that she would have to spend Friday night completing her book work was enough to make her already drooping spirits flag another notch as she unlocked the door and let herself into her apartment. But the most disturbing feeling of all was that something was terribly wrong with Jenny. . . and she would have to drive out tomorrow to see the girl. While she was there, she could talk to Blake about the carnival.

By sheer will and determination, she finished her book work about ten o'clock, slapped the folder shut in triumph and turned on the news. There was a brief but succinct report about the release of the hostages, but it was short and told her nothing she didn't already know. The story of the kidnapping had been given less airtime and was, she supposed, being shifted gradually into the realm of yesterday's news.

Jamie shut off the television and told herself it was really none of her business what Blake Lindstrom had volunteered for, and if Betsy hadn't made herself clear, that was her problem, not Jamie's. But as she got ready for bed and slipped into her nightshirt, the memory of Blake's face when he had discovered he'd been photographed in the act of meeting his daughter appeared inside her head. She couldn't shake it. He'd done everything he could to shun the publicity hounds. Suppose one of them got word of this. They would be all over him again like a swarm of bees. And Jamie would be just as guilty of allowing it to happen as Betsy Bigelow. More so. For Jamie knew two things Betsy didn't know—that Blake was probably unaware of Betsy's choice of jobs for him and that he hated being the center of attention.

A BURR IN THE MIND of a human is like a burr under a horse's saddle, and it makes for equally poor concentration in both critters. Jamie's father had often told her that. When she got up in the morning, she knew it would be much better to drive out to see Blake Lindstrom before she went to the Carson ranch so she would have a clear mind when it was time to practice with Strawberry.

In the end, she compromised. She drove the six miles out of Rock Falls to the Carson ranch, then saddled Strawberry and rode the fifteen more miles west and south that would take her to the Lindstrom place.

It was a fine, fair day for the first week in May, blue sky from one end of the world to the other, a meadowlark trilling a melodious and intricate call. The weather and the countryside and the clean, spring air gave her its well-remembered euphoria. She wore no riding hat. She'd pulled her hair back into a Gypsyish mane, fastened with a leather slide and a wicked-looking pick at the nape of her neck, but the wind, not liking to pass by without leaving a mark, had loosened strands around her face and set them swirling.

It was in this state that she arrived at the ranch, and discovered that the Lindstroms had company. A low, sleek car that had once been pristine white but now was covered with a veil of prairie dust sat in the yard. As if on cue, a woman came out of the house and walked down the three steps toward the car. She was easy for Jamie to see even from a distance, dressed as she was in the same white color as her car. Behind her, the tall form of Blake Lindstrom emerged from the house, his lithe body only a step behind the woman.

A glossy, feminine head lifted in Jamie's direction, as did Lindstrom's. She'd been noticed. Reluctant to intrude, she said a soft word to Strawberry and slowed her to a walk, thinking the woman might get in her car and leave before Jamie arrived at the foot of the steps.

She was not to be so lucky. The woman lingered as if waiting for her. Reluctantly but unable to see how she could delay her arrival any longer, she tethered Strawberry to a hitching post a short distance from the house and began to walk toward Blake and his visitor.

In the morning sun Blake's hair shone like polished coal. He wore a work shirt in regulation blue and jeans that looked as if they'd seen several seasons on the range. A wide, tooled-leather belt set off that lean waist, and under those work-worn jeans his legs looked long, muscled and powerful. He didn't need expensive clothes to heighten his masculinity; quality was inherent in the man.

The nerves at the base of Jamie's throat tightened. Whatever he was thinking was hidden in the cool green depths of those eyes shielded by straight, thick black lashes.

"Hello, Blake," she said, amazed that the words came out as easily as they did.

The woman standing next to the car looked at her long and curiously, her examination just bordering on rudeness, scrutinizing Jamie from her untamed hair to her dusty riding boots. "I thought women like you became extinct when the last one bit the dust on a Hollywood movie lot twenty years ago."

"I assure you, I'm quite real," Jamie said with an exaggerated drawl.

Blake interrupted to make introductions. "Miss Brighton, Miss Gordon. Miss Gordon is Jenny's teacher."

A certain knowledge of women and men and all the variations of their relationships gleamed in the woman's eyes. "Do you make house calls on your pupils, Miss Gordon? Or are you an itinerant teacher in the style of the old circuit-riding preachers?"

Jamie disciplined her face to remain unexpressive. "According to the Geneva convention, I'm only required to give my name, rank and serial number."

It was almost worth being on the receiving end of the woman's needling to see the first genuinely amused smile Jamie had ever seen light up Blake's face.

The elegantly groomed eyebrows lifted. "She is a bright one, isn't she? I thought teachers were supposed to be dull this year."

Blake shook his head. "Ignore her, Jamie. Pauline is a journalist for the magazine, *Pipeline*, and her stock-in-trade is insulting people. That's the way she gets her stories."

The easy way Blake spoke about the woman made Jamie wonder about their relationship. "Maybe she'd like to test her mettle by spending half a day in my classroom," Jamie said crisply.

"I'm smarter than that," said Pauline, smiling at Jamie in a lightning shift of mood that left Jamie dazed. "Are you a friend of Blake's, Miss Gordon?"

"I'm afraid not. We hardly know each other."

"Pity." The woman gave an elaborate sigh. "I was hoping you might use your influence to persuade him to give us an exclusive interview."

"I'm sorry. I have no influence over Mr. Lindstrom."

There was a pause while Pauline pulled an elegant pair of driving gloves from her purse and thrust her hands into them. She lifted her head and favored Jamie with a shrewd, assessing look. "Then why do you ride out to see him before noon on a Saturday?"

"I . . . have something to discuss with him."

"Anything you'd like to share with me?"

"No."

"Clear, crisp and to the point. You prairie people are almost as taciturn as your reputation says you are." Pauline seemed to lose interest in Jamie the moment she turned away. "Blake, darling, if you change your mind, you have my card," she said as she opened the door of the car and slid behind the wheel.

The car disappeared in a cloud of dust, rather like the Wicked Witch of the West had, and over the rising spirals, Jamie's eyes met Blake's. There was a bird singing from a tree in the grove that surrounded the house, and a calf bawled. Time seemed to race and yet stand still.

Jamie waited, and when she saw that he was going to continue to watch her with those eyes and that slight smile lifting his lips, she said dryly, "Should I offer my congratulations?"

"Pauline calls any man darling if she thinks he's going to help her earn that inflated salary she gets." He leaned back, started to fold his arms . . . and stopped. The gesture made Jamie's throat tighten. It was as if he'd made a major concession strictly for her benefit. "To what do I owe the pleasure of your company?"

She was determined not to let him unnerve her, but she wished he weren't standing so close. "I came to see how Jenny is."

There was a slight pause, and then Blake said in an unreadable tone, "She's fine. She'll be back in school next week."

"The doctor didn't find anything seriously wrong?"

"No."

Jamie closed her eyes in relief. "I'm so glad. I was worried—"

"Was that all you wanted to see me about?"

She lifted her head. "No. I wanted to talk to you." She carefully took off her riding gloves and folded them in her hand, her eyes going over his shoulder. From inside the house, she could hear the rattle of dishes. Mrs. Lindstrom was in the kitchen preparing lunch. She stuffed her gloves in her jeans pocket. "Privately, if that's possible."

If he was surprised by her request, he didn't show it. Without hesitating he reached for her elbow and turned her toward the ranch yard. "I'd like to see your horse. Looks like a fine animal."

How simple it would be to talk to him if he didn't have this effect on her. As it was, his hand warmed her flesh and put her brain on disconnect. His nearness made any mental activity an impossibility, except for the sensors that registered his warmth, nearness and maleness.

When they'd reached the roan he ran his hand over the horse's flanks in the way of an experienced horseman, his lean brown fingers following the line of bone and muscle. "Nice horse. About sixteen hands, I'd say. She looks strong and agile. A good combination."

"She needs that combination to get me around those barrels."

He straightened and turned to look at her. "How long have you been barrel racing?"

"Since I was twelve. My father loved the rodeo."

"Any prizes?"

"No. But I'm hoping for a good run or two this season."

"Good luck."

"Thank you." He leaned a little against the horse, obviously waiting. She looked away, at the blue sky, at the land that was his, and told herself that the sooner she got this over with, the better.

"I understand you've volunteered to work at the parent-teacher fair next weekend."

"Yes. You don't approve?"

Why hadn't she foreseen how difficult this would be? "I certainly have no objection to your efforts to be an involved parent, but . . ." She took a breath and realized she had inadvertently stumbled onto the right opening. "But I wonder if you realize just how involved you are."

"I don't think overseeing the duck pond is going to cause any great strain on my talents."

"Betsy isn't going to give you the duck pond. She's planning on having you take charge of . . . the kissing booth."

Those green eyes changed, like the sea rippling. "And you think no one will want to kiss me."

"I don't think anything of the kind. I just didn't want you walking in there Friday night and getting the shock of your life, that's all. You've made it very clear that you despise publicity and—" she gestured toward the lane where the dust raised by the woman journalist's car still hung in the air "—if your friend heard that you'd volunteered to sell kisses at a local fair, she'd reappear instantaneously, and with one wave of her magic white car and her Super Pen, you'd be back in the spotlight."

He seemed to think about it. "But on the other hand, if I tell Miss Bigelow that I've changed my mind and I'm going to go back on my promise, I'm just as likely to be thrust into the spotlight again and look more of a fool than ever. Pauline would love that."

"You don't mean you're going to do it?"

"I don't see that I have much choice." His eyes mocked her, taunted her.

"No, I don't suppose you do." She pushed her hand into her pocket for her gloves, knowing she was angry but not knowing why. She stripped the reins away from the hitching post, turned her back to Blake, thrust a boot into the stirrup and swung into the saddle.

Before she could wheel the horse around, he reached up and caught the pommel. "What's wrong?"

A damnable sunbeam played over his hair as if it belonged there, giving the black hair the polished sheen of a bird's wing. "Nothing."

"Nothing? Are you sure?"

It was a challenge, and her ire rose to meet it. "I thought you didn't like publicity, but it seems that you're more than ready to trade on your newly acquired fame . . . when it suits your purpose."

His face didn't change, but his fingers tightened on the pommel. "Don't judge me."

"Would you please let go?"

"It 'suits my purpose' not to."

His arm brushed her leg, and her nerves tightened. The tension sang through her body, and Strawberry felt it and danced in impatience. Blake said a low word to the horse, and Strawberry went as still as if he'd struck her.

He raised his eyes from the horse to Jamie. "Were you afraid no woman would want to kiss me," he drawled, "or afraid they would?"

"I couldn't care less one way or the other." At Jamie's low, furious tone, Strawberry danced sideways again, but

Blake merely followed the horse. His hold on the pommel stayed firm.

"Miss Bigelow mentioned that the proceeds from the fair will be used to buy books for the library and playground equipment. Maybe I could challenge my uncle to match whatever money I raise."

"Do whatever you like."

His eyes darkened; his mouth lifted in a smile. "Now there," he said, "is an interesting idea."

4

THE NEXT WEEK Blake's daughter returned to school, but it was a little ghost who came through Jamie's classroom door to hang up her sweater on a wall hook and slide listlessly into her desk seat. The girl was a pale, withdrawn imitation of the old vibrant Jenny. Drained of the intensity that was her heritage from Blake, the girl looked less like him than ever. Her brown eyes wary, Jenny turned toward Jamie.

She greeted the girl as normally as she could and decided, for the time being, at least, to say nothing about Jenny's appearance. But she wasn't the only one who had noticed. Several of the little girls in her classroom were casting anxious looks at Jenny.

Striving for a normal tone, Jamie told Jenny she was glad she was feeling better and it was good to have her back. But all through the morning Jamie found her eyes flickering anxiously toward the third seat in the outside row. Where had her bright, happy, enthusiastic Jenny gone?

You're acting like her mother.

From the look of her, she needs one.

Volunteering for the job?

By Wednesday Jamie could stand it no longer. Free of noontime duty, she asked Jenny to stay in and talk with her a bit.

Beforehand Jamie ate her dinner in the faculty room. Spirits there were high, the clowning at its best. Buoyed by the fact that the middle day of the week was half gone by and that there were only three more weeks of school until vacation, the teachers had let the jokes and laughter flow. Jamie, caught up in it all, was late returning to her room. When she walked through her door Jenny was sitting alone, looking small and forlorn among a sea of empty desks.

Stricken with guilt at having made the girl wait, she said, "I'm sorry, Jenny. I should have come sooner."

"It's okay." An image came into her mind, the picture of Jenny, alive, vibrant, waiting for her father to walk into the airport. She'd been so happy. And now . . .

Under Jamie's gaze, Jenny moved restlessly in her seat, the black hair so like Blake's swirling around her shoulders, her brown eyes solemn. Jenny looked across the room out the window, as if watching the children scramble over the jungle gym like monkeys was the most interesting thing in the world for her to be doing at the moment.

Jamie hadn't known this was going to be so hard. Going to the girl, she ached to take her in her arms. Instead she slipped into the desk across the aisle. "Jenny, you haven't been your old self these past few days. Is there . . . is something bothering you?"

A flare of fear came into the girl's eyes. "No," Jenny said, watching Jamie out of the brown depths as wary as a doe's looking at the hunter.

"Please, Jenny. If there's something that's worrying you, I'd like to know what it is. Maybe I can help you."

"Nothing is bothering me." For a few seconds Jenny met Jamie's eyes bravely. Then, as if she could no longer sustain the lie with her eyes as well as her mouth, her gaze flickered away.

Frustrated, wanting very much to help the girl and knowing there was nothing she could do if Jenny didn't see fit to confide in her, except to keep the door open, Jamie smiled. "Well, if you change your mind and think of something you want to share with me, you'll let me know, won't you?"

"Yes, Miss Gordon."

"Fine. Now why don't you get your sweater on and go out and play with the other girls?" Her bright, cheerful dismissal didn't fool Jenny, and Jamie disliked every word as much as she disliked watching Jenny do precisely what she'd told the girl to do, with a listless obedience that tore at the heart.

ON THURSDAY, Jenny was no better.

Friday evening, the day before the fair, Jamie ate a light supper, did some stretching exercises and lay on the floor to relax, preparing herself to go into her bedroom, pick up the phone and call Blake Lindstrom.

When it was nine o'clock and she could put it off no longer, she steeled herself to pick up the receiver. Following his example, she gave Blake no preamble. "I'm calling about Jenny."

There was silence for a moment, as if he didn't recognize her voice at first. Then in that the deep, velvety drawl, "I wondered when I'd be hearing from you."

"What's wrong with her?"

"Nothing we can't work out."

She stood up in stunned silence, holding the phone. How naive she'd been to think the father would be any more forthcoming than the child.

"Blake, I need to know what's wrong. Jenny's school-work is suffering. She still hasn't got all her assignments completed for the week she was gone, and now that she's back, her work is mediocre and she doesn't participate in class discussions at all."

"I'm aware there are problems. We're working on them."

"You're working on them? How? When?"

"Give me another week. If she hasn't improved by then—"

"No. In another week she'll be a wisp of herself. She's not eating, and my guess is she isn't sleeping much, either."

"Astute of you," Blake said grittily.

Another silence, a silence that was meant to make it clear that Blake had no intention of telling her any more than he already had. Driven by desperation and her worry for Jenny, she said, "Have you spent any time with her since you got back or tried to talk with her long enough to find out what's wrong?"

The long, quiet moment stretched. Tension hummed through the telephone wires. Jamie sat clutching the receiver, not caring, recklessly ready to goad him again if he didn't answer her this time.

"I know your opinion of me isn't particularly at its summit . . . but I thought you had acquitted me of child neglect."

"My opinion or nonopinion of you doesn't matter a hoot in hell. It's Jenny who matters—"

"And I'm her father. That gives me the right to decide whether I want to break confidence with my daughter to appease your curiosity."

"It isn't curiosity—"

"Then what would you call it?" the cool voice asked implacably.

"I call it the need to understand and help if I can."

"Understand this: it's my problem, and I'll deal with it. You can 'help' Jenny by treating her normally. Stop singling her out to stay in the classroom and wait for you for several minutes, wondering what she's done wrong and worrying about how much you're going to hate her. Now was there anything else you needed to know?"

Her fury guilt-ridden, she said icily, "No, nothing."

HER ANGER HADN'T COOLED even by Saturday morning, but she drove out to the ranch where Strawberry was stabled, anyway, telling herself it would be good for her to concentrate on her practice.

But all the while she saddled Strawberry, she kept thinking about last night's phone call to Blake. As a communication with a parent, it had been a total failure, and she'd been as much at fault as he. She'd broken every rule. She was emotionally involved with a student, and she'd approached Blake from a less than professional basis.

But how did one approach a man on a professional basis when the sound of his voice brought back memories of the firm sweetness of his mouth? When just hearing him speak made her wonder if she would ever feel that wonderful mouth on hers again?

She might remember that kiss, but she doubted that he did. Blake Lindstrom had a heart made out of rawhide with a coating as tough as armadillo skin. He'd kissed her once, but he'd probably banished it from his mind the moment she'd walked out of the stable.

What had he meant when he'd said he knew her opinion of him wasn't high? Had he taken the allegory about the man in the mask to heart? If he had, she hadn't noticed any softening, particularly when he thought she was meddling in something that wasn't her business.

Jamie had hoped that the fresh air and the sunshine and the smell of the alfalfa in the field would lift her spirits, but her practice session wasn't one of her better ones. She was simply going through the motions, pushing Strawberry to a faster pace around the barrels, but she wasn't concentrating. It would be much smarter to quit. Lack of concentration could lead to an accident.

She turned the horse around and headed toward the stable, holding an impatient Strawberry, who knew exactly where they were going, to a slow trot. Jamie could almost hear the mare thinking about her carrot treat.

She rounded the corner of the stable, and someone stepped out of the doorway. A woman.

"Mrs. Lindstrom," Jamie murmured, sliding out of the saddle, trying to think what she had done to merit this visit from Ruth.

Caught in the sunlight, the strands of gray in hair the same black as her son's shone like silver. She wore a light blue cotton dress; with her tall, slim body, and her high cheekbones, she might have been envied by a model. As Ruth walked toward her with a graceful gait particularly suited to the rough ground of the alfalfa field, Jamie could see how this woman had engendered the admiration of the two Lindstrom brothers for most of a lifetime.

"Do you have a few moments?" Ruth asked.

"Yes, of course. Why don't you come in the stable, and we'll talk while I'm rubbing her down?" She raised a hand and laid it on Strawberry's flank. The horse sidestepped and whickered low in her throat.

Jamie led the mare into the stall, scooped some oats into the feeding trough and picked up a soft cloth to begin rubbing Strawberry's flanks.

"She's a fine-looking horse."

"Yes, she is." Jamie worked, determined that this time she was going to practice a little discretion, something she found it easier to do with Ruth than with Blake.

Ruth seemed to be gathering herself. "I came to see you today because I . . . overheard my son's half of the conversation the night you called. Unlike my son, I think we need your help." She paused, took a breath. "I don't know what your relationship is with Blake, but he had no right to talk to you that way. It's just that he hasn't been himself since . . . and he's very worried about Jenny. When we had the doctor out, he could find nothing physically wrong with her. He recommended we . . ." Ruth stopped and in the shadowy stable, the only sound Jamie could hear was the woman's breathing and her own rhythmic swipe over Strawberry's hide.

"He recommended that we take her to a psychiatrist."

Jamie felt as if she'd been punched in the stomach. "Why?" She turned to face Ruth and saw the pain in the other woman's eyes.

"She has this idea that if she lets Blake out of her sight, he'll go away again and not come back. That's why she wouldn't go to school. For those first few days, after Blake finally got her to tell him what was wrong, he took her with him everywhere. She rode out on the range with him, over to Sioux Falls when he went for supplies. At night, he slept on a chair in her room so that if she woke, he'd be there."

The picture of Blake, exhausted, his lean frame sprawled on a too-small chair next to Jenny's bed brought a lump to Jamie's throat. "Was there something that brought this on?"

"Two things, actually. The first night Blake was home, Jenny woke up and went looking for him. He wasn't in his bed. He couldn't sleep and had ridden out on the range. She was almost hysterical by the time he came back. Then Blake told her about having to go away for an operation. That was when she began to pretend she was sick so she could stay home from school to be with him."

"What is he going to do?"

"He's canceled the operation, temporarily, at least. He'll have it done eventually, of course, but by not going in when he's scheduled to, he'll fall off the priority list, and he'll have to wait longer than two weeks after he does schedule."

Jamie closed her eyes. It was a nightmare, this chain reaction to Blake's captivity.

"My son tends to be too . . . independent. He's adamant about not seeing a psychiatrist. If there is anything you can do to help Jenny, I'd appreciate it. And Blake will, too, believe me."

"I'm not sure I can do anything about Jenny's feelings toward her father, but I'll try in every way I can to reassure her that her dad's home to stay."

"Thank you. I thought if you understood about Jenny, you might see why Blake is so . . . abrasive."

"Yes, I do see. And I appreciate your coming and telling me this very much."

"I just wanted you to see that— I'm not sure who needs understanding more, Jenny or her father."

"Yes," Jamie said thoughtfully, watching as Ruth turned to go.

"IF RIDING IN RODEOS makes your legs look like that, I want to start," Tiki said. "What's the first thing I need to learn?"

"To watch where you step," Jamie said dryly. "That's the first rule everybody learns who works with horses." Maybe this was what they all needed, a night to be totally foolish, to dress in silly costumes and forget. . . .

She wished she could forget the things she'd said to Blake. She'd been wrong, so wrong. She'd accused him of not communicating with his daughter, even while he'd been taking her with him everywhere. He was a hard man with an armor of steel, but for Jenny there was a very large chink in it. Could such a devoted father really be incapable of loving someone else?

Who did you have in mind as a candidate?

Forget it. Just . . . forget it.

If she needed silly costumes to help her take her mind off Blake, there could hardly be a sillier costume in the world than the one Tiki was wearing. She was almost lost inside a too-large pink bunny suit with floppy feet and a hood of large ears. Tufts of fiery red hair peeked from under the circle of pink fur. Her elfin face brought into sharp focus, her sparkling brown eyes full of mischief, she looked the unlikeliest Easter Bunny west of the Mississippi.

Dressed in her brief costume with its minuscule, stick-out skirt, Jamie stood on one long, elegantly curved leg and propped the other on her dressing table bench to reach under and twist the seam of her net stocking into a semblance of a straight line.

"Did I mention, Jamie, that by the end of the evening those things make your legs look as if you spent the night rolled up in a tennis racket?"

"No, you didn't mention that. But after having them on for a few minutes, I could have guessed."

"I have to give you credit," Tiki said, sitting up and playing casually with the pink mitts that she hadn't yet put on. "I thought you'd probably develop a sudden, inexplicable tropical fever tonight."

"I looked through the encyclopedia today, trying to find just the right one." Jamie kept her face mock serious. "None of them allowed for instant recovery the next morning." She lowered her high-heeled shoe to the floor, felt the pull of the net stocking along her thigh and wondered if they would last the evening. If they didn't, her costume wouldn't cover up the hole. The skirt didn't have enough material in it to make a place mat, and there wasn't much more to the top. She gave the sweetheart neckline a tug upward and sighed. The dress was blue satin and came with shoes to match. Her legs looked sexy and endless. Would the parents of her students understand that she was doing this for a good cause? Of course, it was a fun night for everyone, and the teachers traditionally let their hair down. But she'd put hers up, and she felt as if she were all neck and legs. Tiki had gathered the chestnut strands into a Victorian topknot with lots of sprigged curls pulled down around her face and neck, as well as having painted her lips a voluptuous red in the best forties-movie style. "I look like a cross between Betty Grable and Shirley Temple."

Tiki put her head back to give Jamie a critical look. "The Betty Grable I can see. The Shirley Temple takes a wee bit more imagination." Tiki's eyes lingered briefly at Jamie's well-shaped breasts, so luxuriously outlined by the satin. "What are you going to do about the kissing booth occupant?"

Jamie shook her head. "You think I know?" Her mouth twisted in a wry smile. "I'd a thousand times rather be saddling up to a barrel race on muddy turf than this."

"You can't mean that, not really. Slopping around in all that slush?"

"It would be easier than this. Riding, you're dealing with a horse you know better than any human being in the world and a turf you've walked over. You're keeping the unknowns to a minimum. But this—" her slim shoulders moved under the brief costume "—there aren't any rules."

"Yes, there are. There's that most basic rule of all. Woman, watch out for thy heart, lest thee lose it to the wrong man."

"Thank you, Oracle Jones."

The bunny ears flopped forward in a comic bow. "I give excellent advice that no one, least of all me, pays any attention to."

"Does that mean you're giving up on Drew?"

"Yes . . . until the next time I see him."

Casually, examining a fingernail, Jamie said, "What about Bill Halbrook?"

Tiki's head came up. "What about him?"

"He's asked you out a few times. Why don't you go?"

"Maybe because I don't want to. Listen, don't talk to me about Bill Halbrook. That cowboy is looking for a woman who's a combination round-the-clock short-order cook, sheep midwife and ranch hand."

"You think he only loves you for your energy?"

"He doesn't love me at all. He just enjoys—" Tiki frowned, looking fiercely intent "—dreaming the impossible dream. And I think he's found the ultimate mirage in that scrubby ranch of his. Thanks, but no thanks. I want to teach school, not nursemaid a bunch of bleating sheep. They're not the most intelligent animals in the world, you know."

"So you've told me before."

Fitting her hands into the pink mitts shaped to look like rabbit paws, Tiki stood up. "Let's just forget it. Come on. If you do anything else to look more beautiful, I won't leave chocolate eggs in your Easter basket—you'll get stones."

Outside, in the dusk-soft early evening, the spring air was cool against Jamie's net-covered legs. She clipped along in her high heels, while beside her, Tiki shuffled, the only step her oversized rabbit suit allowed.

"Now I know why rabbits hop," she grumbled. "They sure can't walk. I'll never laugh at a bunny again."

"Well, you know what they say about walking a mile in a man's moccasins. I suppose that applies to rabbit's feet, as well."

"Please, spare me the poor philosophy. We *are* early enough to get into the gym without anyone seeing us, aren't we? What is that noise?" A rabbit paw clutched Jamie's arm. "Good grief, look."

They had rounded the corner, and in the soft light of the setting sun they saw a line of people waiting to get into the school. The line snaked around the corner of the building.

"It pays to advertise, doesn't it?" Tiki muttered. "The whole darned state must have heard about the kissing cousin."

Jamie stepped on a tiny pebble, and her high heel wobbled. She stumbled and would have fallen if Tiki hadn't had such a grip on her arm. Tiki gave her a sharp look. "Your moccasins aren't doing too well by you tonight. Want to try mine?"

"No, thanks."

The gym blazed with lights. Colored balloons were strung everywhere like bright, overblown jelly beans. She was reminded of a riverboat she'd once seen outfitted for a Fourth of July celebration. The gym looked ready to set sail, awash with tissue-paper carnations and gaiety.

None of the booths were manned yet. The kissing booth sat squarely in the middle of the floor. Around it, against the wall, were the games, set up and waiting, the beanbag toss, the basketball toss, the putting green and the so-called duck pond. George the duck was already there, looking appropriately daffy since a real duck had been procured for the event, swimming round and round in Jennifer Clark's little sister's kiddie pool.

Jamie, following Tiki's rabbit ears, ducked through the doorway into the room off the gym used for the concession stand during the games, the room that smelled perpetually of caramel corn. Someone, she wasn't sure who, was supposed to provide her with her ersatz cigarette tray and the candies and gum that she would be selling.

The tiny room was mass confusion. Tom Coachman was filling beanbags, Drew was searching for the prizes to be given away at the duck pond and Betsy looked more distracted than ever.

"Blake will be a little late," Drew murmured to Jamie. "He's out counting cattle noses. He thinks he may have had some more stolen."

"He needs that like another hole in the head—" Jamie stopped, stricken.

A look crossed Drew's face, an expression of startled amusement.

"I didn't mean—"

Drew laughed softly. "Of course you didn't. Relax, sweetheart. You're strung up as tightly as those stockings of yours." He gave her a closer perusal, a once over lightly that was complimentary but not leering, as if he could sense her self-consciousness. "Although I must say, you make a very attractive package."

Somebody overheard Drew and laughed. Jamie had vowed she wasn't going to let anything anybody said or did on this night bother her, but she felt her cheeks warm. Drew rewarded her for blushing by leaning over and giving her a kiss on the cheek.

"Hey," Tiki protested from under her pink hood, "freebies not allowed on school premises tonight."

"I'm feeling reckless right at the moment."

A peculiar silence fell over the room. The group's eyes shifted beyond Jamie. Everyone was looking at the doorway.

Jamie turned . . . and saw Blake looking at her with that cool, hard, half beautiful, half tragic face. No one moved or spoke, and Jamie realized then that she wasn't alone in her feelings about Blake. In any group he was an unknown factor, an alien. It was more than the scar on his face; it was his attitude, his bearing. People sensed he was a man to be wary of. He had seen too much, suffered too much, to be bound by polite social rules.

But overlying the dangerously controlled, contorted mask was fatigue. He looked exhausted. Jamie thought of him, sleeping in the chair by his daughter's bedside, and her heart went out to him. His eyes flickered back to hers, and his face became more austere, wintry, his body stiff with pride and control.

He stepped farther into the room, his glacial gaze searching for Betsy Bigelow. "I'm sorry I'm late."

Afterward she didn't know whether it was the expression on Drew's face or Blake's quiet, dark voice with its faint note of strain that drove her toward him. She only knew that she couldn't go on standing there thinking about all he had done for his daughter, watching as he stood alone facing the cluster of teachers as if he were an outnumbered enemy.

"You're not that late. We're just glad you're here." His faintly surprised expression made her bold. In that quiet room, with everyone watching, she took the two steps that put her directly in front of him and turned laughing eyes up to him. "Maybe you should practice before you begin your work assignment."

He caught her arms and braced his elbows, stopping her in midflight and holding her away. "What makes you think I need practice?"

Startled, she looked up at him, and the cool indifference in his face brought the bright sting of blood to her cheeks. Yet she was closer to him than she had been before. Her tiny puffed-out skirt was crushed against his hips, and his chest was a hairsbreadth from hers. Slowly, inexplicably, he pulled her closer, as if his hands had a will of their own, undeterred by the message of remote reserve she saw in his face. Their bodies touched lightly, briefly, at chest and thigh, and while she watched, the green eyes changed. The sea rippled, and something new surfaced, something far from indifference and decidedly dangerous.

He's changed his mind. He's going to kiss you, after all. . . .

A strong, masculine hand cupped her nape, and another shaped itself to her hip. She was brought lovingly up to his mouth, like a treasure to be savored before the plundering. Yet he still didn't kiss her. He held her there, watching. Watching for what? She didn't know. She only knew his mouth was a tantalizing few inches away, and she could feel her body straining for completion of what was now, must be, had to be, inevitable.

Blake knew this was madness. He'd meant to hold her off with a polite, quick play on words. He hadn't wanted to line up behind his cousin for a kiss from her. But when she'd stepped close to him and offered him her mouth, he'd found himself pulling her closer instead of pushing her away, watching her for some sign of distaste as she looked at his scarred face. There was none. There was nothing in her eyes but the dazed look of a woman waiting to be kissed.

There were too many people watching; it was the wrong time and the wrong place. . . .

He muttered something, a soft, satisfied word unintelligible to Jamie's ears but that seemed to be a response to the feel of her in his hands, and lowered his mouth to hers.

His lips were warm, pliant, inviting. They brushed Jamie's in an unsatisfying silken meeting, a smoothly rhythmic pass, gone almost before her mouth had softened to accommodate their lovely shape and feel. She lifted her hands, intent on stopping that disturbing drift of his head, when she found herself being held away, and then, standing alone.

"My thanks for practicing with me." He bowed his head slightly, an old-fashioned gesture of respect that held the faintest touch of mockery. When the dark head came up again, his eyes were brilliant. "I'm sure my future customers will appreciate your efforts on their behalf."

Dazed, Jamie turned away to find Drew watching avidly. As Blake moved past Jamie to talk to Betsy Bigelow, asking if there was anything he should be doing or any special costume she wanted him to wear, the two cousins stood caught in Jamie's vision like opposite sides of a coin. Drew faced her with a faint smile on his lips. Blake's back was ramrod straight with pride. Drew wore a bright turquoise shirt in a flamboyant cotton print; Blake's broad shoulders were clad in dove-gray silk that rippled when he moved and caught the light like pearl. With his back to her and his full head of dark hair brushed and cut to curl over his collar, his waist indented and marked by a sleek leather belt, he looked every woman's ideal. If only. . . If only. . . what? Did she want Blake to be more like Drew? But if he were, he wouldn't be the man who'd gone to the defense of two women at the risk of his life.

Blake looked the way he did because of what he was. And she liked what he was. She liked it very much. And yet there was that dark side of Blake, that uncontrolled side, the side that frightened her.

Slowly, as if Jamie were a pupil of his that he was warning away from danger, Drew shook his head from side to side.

Annoyed, and not sure whether she was irritated with Drew or with herself for being so transparent, she picked up the tray laden with candy, packages of peanuts and gum and bent her head to slide the broad satin ribbon around her neck.

Drew materialized beside her, and as his fingers helped her adjust the weight of the tray, he leaned over and said in a low tone close to her ear, "You're playing with fire, sweet."

She straightened and met his chiding look with a cool one. "I can take care of myself."

"I very much doubt that. But we shall see."

Was it minutes or hours later when the doors opened and the noise level in the gym exploded from quiet to unbearably deafening? Jamie didn't know. But as she walked around holding a package of peanuts in her hand in an attempt to persuade people to buy, it seemed as if the minutes were hours. The brick walls reverberated with the groans of disappointed children, who tried to toss embroidery hoops over George's neck and missed; with protesting quacks from George; with ecstatic shouts from children who managed to score three baskets in a row and win a prize.

Jamie walked a wide circle around the duck pond. She was too aware of the temptation she would be to George. When she'd walked out of the tiny room where Blake had kissed her, Betsy had raced after her waving the candy bracelets for Jamie to wear, bright candies strung on elastic. Betsy had slipped the first one over Jamie's arm and, dangling the second in her fingers, had said, "Be a good sport and wear this one around your ankle, won't you? It will make you look so authentic. Thanks, Jamie, you're a doll."

She felt like a doll, the walking, windup kind. She handed out candy and made change, but her mind wasn't on what she was doing. The sweetness of Blake's mouth on her lips and the memory of the way his hands had fitted themselves to the curve of her nape and the bone of her hip lingered around her like a cloud of smoke. That memory, and the reality of him standing behind the flimsy barrier of paper that comprised the bottom part of the kissing booth, leaning out to press his lips lightly on yet another female paying customer, gave Jamie a feeling of being caught in a time trap that was neverending.

He certainly doesn't look as if he's suffering.

She turned away and was making another circuit past the duck pond when a tug at her skirt brought her head around. Jenny stood close to her, her eyes bright. "Hi, Miss Gordon."

Glad for the diversion the child provided, Jamie squatted and balanced the clumsy box on her knees. "Hello, sweetheart. Having a good time?"

"Yes. See what I won?" Solemnly Jenny proffered a small, stuffed brown bear for Jamie's inspection. The brown eyes were not so wary tonight, and there was a little color in her cheeks. Distracted by the carnival, she looked almost normal again.

"Good for you. That's a really nice prize."

"My daddy's having a good time, too, isn't he? He's smiling a lot more than he usually does." The child turned to gaze toward the booth where Blake stood putting the money Jennifer Clark's mother had given him in the money box and wiping dark red lipstick from his mouth. Behind Mrs. Clark, Tiki stood in line, for what had to be, Jamie thought, the third time.

She swallowed past the lump in her throat. Why had she been afraid no one would want to kiss Blake? "Maybe he has more reason to smile than usual."

"I guess he likes kissing everybody."

Isn't that the truth? "I guess he does." *But he didn't want to kiss you. He was going to stop you. Then he took pity on you and gave you a half kiss, one you'd very much like to finish....*

"Have you bought a kiss from my daddy yet?" Jenny looked up at Jamie with all the innocence of her youth.

"No, I haven't."

"Why not?"

Out of the mouths of babes. Why not, indeed? "Because the tray would get in the way and spill, and we'd have chocolate candy and peanuts and gum all mixed up together."

Jenny gave her a shy smile, the first one Jamie could remember seeing on the girl's lips in a long while. "I guess you would. But it's not fair. You should get a chance just like everybody else." She frowned, thinking about it until her face suddenly brightened. "I know what. I'll hold the tray while you go buy a kiss from my daddy."

"Well, thank you very much, Jenny, but I'm afraid the tray is too big for you."

"Then we'll set it on the floor, and I'll just watch it."

"No, really, I—I couldn't. I have to sell all the candy first." Jamie straightened in preparation to extract herself from Jenny's determination . . . only to find Blake, unoccupied at the moment, staring at his daughter . . . and at her.

Jenny saw him, too. "Hi, Daddy," she said, running on tiptoe toward him. And into a sudden, rare moment of quiet the child piped, "I was trying to get Miss Gordon to let me watch her tray so she could come and kiss you, but she said she couldn't."

At the exact same time, George decided he'd dodged his last embroidery hoop—enough was enough. He poked his head over the rim of the swimming pool and tumbled headlong onto the gym floor. With a loud, protesting quack and a disgruntled ruffle of his feathers, he gathered his feet under him and headed straight for Jamie.

Everything seemed to take on a nightmare reality then. She felt as if her muscles had gone liquid, incapable of movement, and she could do nothing but stand and watch.

George, enthralled by the sight of the brightly colored candies circling Jamie's ankle, decided he was hungry and that those looked quite appetizing. He gave a garbled quack and pecked at Jamie's leg.

More startled than frightened, sounding a little like George, she cried out and did a dance, trying to balance her heavy tray and fend off George. She couldn't. Duck-like, he was single-minded in his determination to gobble a sweet, his wide bill poking at a considerable part of Jamie's net-covered leg.

The south end of her tray, piled with candy bars, was heavier than the north end filled with gum and peanuts. The tray tilted and became a slide that sent the candy bars slithering into the water. Jamie cried out, grabbed for them, got tangled in the ribbon of her tray, stumbled over George, thought she'd stepped on him, hopped back and lost her balance, only to teeter and fall sideways into Jennifer Clark's little sister's wading pool.

A woman shrieked, water splashed and Jamie felt a sharp pain in her thigh. She lay unable to move, afraid to move, trying to wipe the water from her eyes when she saw Blake reach out with a firm hand, snatch George around his yellow legs and hand him off to Drew. In the same fluid motion he reached for her, slipped the soggy satin ribbon from around her neck, grasped her hand and brought her up out of the pond.

"Wouldn't it have been easier just to come over and kiss me?" Muted amusement at her predicament gleamed in his eyes.

"I wasn't— I didn't—"

"Shh. I know. It's all right. I was only teasing you."

His beautiful shirt was covered with splotches of water that seemed to have come from her. "I'm getting you all wet," she said in a throaty voice that was close to breaking.

"I'll dry. Come on. Let's get you somewhere away from this carnival of errors."

He put his arm around her, and suddenly it didn't seem so bad to be dripping every step of the way across the floor in front of most of the community of Rock Falls. The warmth of him soothed; the strength of him protected. All the while they walked that long, long way across the floor, there wasn't a sound. It was only after they were almost to the door that a rumble of laughter began, followed by a snicker or two. Drew's voice broke through the laughter. "Great. He gets the girl—and I get stuck with the duck."

"You gotta get faster on the draw, Drew," some wise-acre teased, and that was the last thing Jamie heard. They were out into the cool night together, she and Blake, and he was putting her into his car.

"Uh-uh," he said at the look at her eyes as he opened the door. "Don't tell me you'll get the seat of the car all wet. I don't give a damn."

"I can walk. It's only a short way—"

"Get in."

She got in.

"Tell me where you live."

She told him.

When they reached her apartment and he saw the stairs, he said, "Sit still and wait for me. I'll come around and get you and carry you up."

"There's no need—"

"You could barely walk across the gym floor, you were hurting so badly. There's a need."

She sat still.

He carried her up the stairs and continued to hold her while she unlocked the door. Inside her apartment, he glanced around. "I'll help you out of that thing you're wearing. Where's the bathroom?"

Inside his arms, she stiffened, and her face grew chilly. "I don't need any help."

He stared down at her, the slender woman he held like a child, and for a long moment their eyes met, and his will clashed with hers. To her amazement, he nodded. "All right. Is your robe inside your door?"

"Yes."

He carried her into the bathroom and let her feet slide gently to the floor. He looked around, pulled the towel off the rack and laid it on the counter near her. Her robe he put on the other side.

"If you feel faint, for God's sake, call me."

She gave him a straight look. "I will."

Her net stockings and wet clothes piled in the sink, her body showered, towel-dried and wrapped in her robe, she came out of the bathroom, knowing he was still in the apartment.

When she came into the room, he turned, and for a moment his eyes were unprotected, dark with feeling. She felt as if she were seeing Blake as he had once been, younger, vulnerable, caring. But while she watched, his face assumed its normal, self-contained expression. She asked, "Would you like some coffee?"

"Don't be a fool. You're favoring that right hip. Lie down and let me see if you've broken something."

"I'm all right—"

His head came up then, and those eyes took fire with an emotion she'd never seen before. "Are you afraid to let me touch you?"

"No, of course not, but—"

"Then come and lie down."

There was a long, quiet moment in the apartment, but at last her eyes fell before his. She limped to the couch and winced as she tried to lie down. Blake looked peculiar, as if he were suffering pain, but he made no move to help her until she was reclining against the pillow.

He knelt beside the couch, and arranging her robe carefully over her thigh, he ran his hands along the length of her leg, down over her knee and ankle. He moved to do the same to the other one, but when his hand traveled along her right thigh, she winced. He said nothing, his eyes intent on the downward path of his hands.

"Which leg did George bite? I want to see if he broke the skin."

"He didn't. He—"

"Which, Jamie?"

"The right one." He was impatient, intent on examining her flesh, unaware that he'd called her by her first name.

"No broken skin. You won't need a tetanus shot." He traced a thumb over a criss-cross line left by her stocking.

Open your heart to love with 4 Best Seller Romances FREE

Can you resist the promise of wild, passionate romance...the shy glances, the stolen kisses, the laughter – and the tears? If, deep within your heart, you're a true romantic, then these are love stories for you. Stories that comprise a unique library of books from Mills & Boon – we call them Best Seller Romances. From the very first page you'll understand why these books have enthralled thousands of readers and now rank among our Best Sellers.

As your special introduction to our most popular library, we'll send you 4 Best Sellers, an exclusive Digital Quartz Clock and a surprise mystery gift absolutely FREE when you complete and return this card.

Now, if you decide to become a subscriber, you can receive four Best Seller Romances delivered directly to your door, every two months. If this sounds tempting, read on; because you'll also enjoy a whole range of special benefits that are exclusive to Mills & Boon. For example, a free bi-monthly newsletter packed with recipes, competitions, exclusive book offers and much more – plus extra bargain offers and big cash savings.

Remember, there's absolutely no obligation or commitment – you can cancel your subscription at any time. So don't delay any longer...complete, detach and post this card today. The romance of your dreams is beckoning – don't keep it waiting!

PLUS A QUARTZ CLOCK and a Mystery Gift

FREE BOOKS CERTIFICATE

Dear Susan,

Your special Introductory Offer of 4 Free books is too good to miss. I understand they are mine to keep with the Free Clock and mystery gift. Please also reserve a Reader Service Subscription for me. If I decide to subscribe I shall receive 4 new books every two months for £7.80 post and packing free. If I decide not to subscribe, I shall write to you within 10 days. The free books and gifts will be mine to keep, in any case.

I understand that I may cancel or suspend my subscription at any time simply by writing to you. I am over 18 years of age.   2A8B

_____ Signature _____

Name _____
(BLOCK CAPITALS PLEASE)

Address _____

_____ Postcode _____

To Susan Welland
Mills & Boon Reader Service
FREE POST
P.O. Box 236
CROYDON
Surrey CR9 9EL

SEND NO MONEY NOW

"Does Ralph Nader know about these things?" She smiled at him, and he gave her a smile back that made her heart turn over. As if he sensed the shared intimacy and wanted to reject it, he sobered and said in a cool tone, "My guess is you strained a muscle in your thigh, trying to save yourself when you fell. You'd better take it easy the next few days—don't do any riding." He looked up and caught her eyes on him, and misread what he saw there. His face took on its usual wintry look. "Unless you're not satisfied with my diagnosis . . ."

"I'm perfectly satisfied with your diagnosis. I'm sure you made it as you do everything else, with great thoroughness and expertise. I was only thinking about what a disaster this whole evening has been. I'll lose a week of practice . . . and I've ruined your shirt. It's all wet."

"I'll survive."

He tossed off the words as a polite man would, but in the silence of the room they took on a deeper meaning.

"You'll survive. . . . 'To live and laugh another day'?" Jamie slanted a look at him, her heart pounding, her nerves clamoring at her temerity. "When are you going to start living and laughing again, Blake?"

His face suddenly devoid of emotion, he said, "Is there anything else you want?"

Yes. I want you to be whole again.

"No. Nothing."

Again that nineteenth-century drop of the head. It would haunt her dreams, that bow. "I understand, believe me, I do. No, don't get up. I'll lock the door on my way out."

5

"I DON'T LIKE to see you doing this." Tiki was sprawled on her stomach on Jamie's bed, her chin propped in her hands while she watched Jamie hobble around the room.

Jamie sat down on the vanity bench in front of her mirror, lifted her leg to pull on a riding boot and winced. Her thigh was hurting badly, and she hadn't been able to hide how she felt from Tiki. With elaborate care she tucked the bottom of her pant leg into the boot. "You're repeating yourself, teacher."

"Call them up and tell them you're not coming. You're in no shape to ride."

Jamie shook her head. "I promised Ruth I would come, and I can't go back on my word to her, not when Jenny has actually agreed to leave her father for an hour and let me show her how to run a course around the barrels. That's a big step forward for her."

"She saw you take that dive into the duck pond, and she's a bright girl. She'll understand that you're hurting—"

Jamie shook her head. "No. I can't run the risk of disappointing her. I'll be all right. We probably won't stay out long."

Tiki sat up and crossed her denim-covered legs under her, her energetic action making Jamie's bed shake. "Well, if you ask me, this is going way beyond the call of duty. I could see it when Blake was gone, but he's back now and—"

"I can't stop being Jenny's friend now just because he's home, when she still needs my help. Hand me my hat, would you?"

"You're the one who needs help," Tiki said gruffly, reaching for the hat and tossing it through the air to her, watching as Jamie caught it and threaded the string around her neck. "You're an absolute sucker for an unhappy kid."

"While you have a heart of iron—"

"My heart is in perfectly good shape. Have you looked at yours lately?"

Jamie faced her friend and plunged straight into the verbal battle. "You aren't by any chance referring to Blake Lindstrom, are you?"

"Not by chance, by malice aforethought."

"He's not interested in me."

"Oh?" Tiki raised an eyebrow. "He just makes it a habit to collect half-wet women out of pools and carry them up to their apartments, is that it?"

"He probably felt obligated because I'm Jenny's friend."

"Listen, lady. I've been teaching school a little longer than you have, and no man has ever looked at me like that because I've been a friend to his child. I urge caution here. Lindstrom has heartbreaker written all over him in six-foot-three-inch-tall letters."

"You didn't look very cautious last Saturday night, standing in line waiting to kiss him."

Tiki looked unabashed. "Sure, I'll admit it. I made a play for him. What sane woman wouldn't? But I'd never be naive enough to fall for him. While you, on the other hand—you lead with your heart."

Jamie shook her head. "I'd love to stay and listen to this fascinating psychological analysis, but I've got to go."

Tiki shrugged and climbed off the bed. "Never say you weren't warned."

Later, as Jamie sat on her horse watching Jenny ride her own fleet-footed little mare, Fair Lady, around the barrels in the pattern that Jamie had traced, she was glad she hadn't listened to Tiki. Jenny had looked apprehensive when she'd ridden over to the practice field, Ruth beside her. Now the child radiated delight. The fresh air, the exercise and her own intent concentration on the things Jamie had told her had chased the clouds from Jenny's eyes. The dark red windbreaker the girl wore was open and billowing behind her, and the wind lifted her dark hair and brought a sheen to her cheeks. For a few moments, at least, she had forgotten her worries about her father and looked as a child should look, raptly involved, happy.

When Jenny completed the pattern, Jamie nodded encouragingly. "Both you and Fair Lady are starting to look very good. Try leaning toward the barrels just a little more as you go around them. Then pick up speed when you go for the straightaway. I think if we had some different shoes on your Lady, she could really show us some speed."

"Do you think Daddy would let me get her shoes changed? He always says I have too many pairs."

Seated on her horse, Jamie grinned. "If he objects to your horse having an extra pair, just tell him she needs them because she has twice as many feet as you do."

It wasn't a sterling piece of wit, but Jenny was obviously in the mood to laugh, and she did it enthusiastically, her head thrown back in enjoyment. When she had sobered a little, Jenny looked beyond Jamie's shoulder. Jamie wondered what it was she saw. The sun was dropping lower on the horizon, and the soft light cast shadows across the prairie. "I could ask him right now," Jenny said excitedly. "He's coming to ride home with me."

Resisting the urge to turn around, Jamie grasped the pommel and shifted in her saddle, the reins lying loosely in her hands. "Well, he certainly timed that just right, didn't he?" Unable to keep her back to him any longer, she lifted the reins and turned the mare in a half circle.

Man and horse were one dark figure outlined against a pale peach sky. He rode closer, and Jamie found herself holding her breath. Under his hat his face was shadowed, and his clothing was a part of his dark figure, indiscernible.

Closer he came, and when he was near enough for Jamie to see the thrust of his jaw under that broad brim, she braced herself.

He brought his horse alongside hers. "Are you sure you should be riding?" His voice was low, pitched so Jenny couldn't hear.

"I'm all right."

"Are you?" There was a strange tone in his voice, a velvety promise that seemed to match the slate-gray blueness of the evening. "Yes, I think you are. You are very much all right, Jamie Gordon. After what I said to you the other night, I didn't deserve your concern."

"Perhaps you don't," Jamie replied, knowing she didn't mean it. "But Jenny does."

A faint, rare smile from Blake. Amazing how much lighter her heart felt when she saw that smile. "And you're not about to let one recalcitrant cowboy get in the way of what you set out to do, are you?"

"Never." In the last rays of the dying sun, she smiled back at him.

Did she imagine the sudden sexual tension that seemed to vibrate between them, his slight shifting in the saddle in response? She must have. "I suppose I'd better take my daughter home." His voice held a darker tone, a faint huskiness. Had he been wondering, just as she had, what would happen if she were as determined to bring him happiness as she was his daughter?

"I suppose you'd better," she said lightly.

He hesitated, wanting to say something. "As I rode up, I heard you both laughing. I realized then that I hadn't heard Jenny laugh since I came home. I— Thank you for not getting angry when I gave you those rather rude instructions on the phone. Thank you for not withdrawing your friendship from Jenny," he said gravely, his eyes still hidden by the brim of his hat.

Jamie's throat filled with emotion. He was a big man, big enough to admit he'd made a mistake. "You're welcome."

THE NEXT MORNING, Thad Lindstrom sat heavily in the saddle, his eyes scanning the flat South Dakota horizon. "Get yourself to a plastic surgeon, boy, and have that face fixed."

Blake knew why his uncle didn't meet his eyes. He wouldn't have dared.

Blake studied the sky, the white clouds scattered like random mountains over the blue. He was used to being badgered by his uncle. When he spoke his voice was low, controlled. "I can't leave Jenny right now, Thad."

Storm pawed the ground restlessly, but it was a bid for attention more than a request to get moving. The stallion was calmer now after his run. Minutes ago, out riding on a fence-inspection tour with his uncle, Blake had felt restless, and he'd given the stallion free rein. They'd taken off like the wind and reached the Peak long before Thad, mounted on the bay gelding, had puffed up behind them. The Peak was the name they'd jokingly given the only hill on the ranch.

Blake looked out over his land and cattle and told himself he wouldn't let his uncle ruin his enjoyment of this rare moment of relaxation. For the past week he'd been getting ready for the spring roundup, constructing the temporary pens, checking the branding table, buying the medicine from the vet. Everything happened at once in early summer. To complicate matters, he'd had to do his fieldwork while Jenny was in school, then plan how to carry hay to the steers and repair the baler when she was around so that he could keep her with him. No rest for the wicked. God knew, he must be wicked. He'd run himself into the ground, working, staying with Jenny at night. It hadn't helped him forget the sound of Jamie's laughter, and her face filled with compassion. Nothing had helped.

"Hell and damnation." His uncle leaned to one side of his horse and spat onto the ground. "Take your little gal with you. You can afford it. You're the only man I know who isn't up to his hind end in debt to the bank and borrowing more money to live on."

"Lessons learned at my father's knee," Blake said quietly.

Thad scowled. "And at mine. And at mine." He shook his head, took off his hat, untying the kerchief around his neck, wiped his brow. "I've never known you to be a quitter. What happened to you?"

"Think it's going to rain, Uncle?" Blake asked blandly.

"I think it's going to pour pitchforks and hammer handles—or maybe I'm just gonna end up throwing them at you. You're hiding behind that scar, boy."

This was too much of an echo of the things Jamie had said, too close to the bone. Blake turned to look his uncle in the eye. "You've been reading too much science fiction."

Thad's hard gaze never wavered. "I've never known you to turn coward before."

For a moment Blake's mouth tightened. Then he turned his head to let his eyes take in the pristine colors of blue and green and the rusty red backs of his cattle. "Am I tarnishing my image for you?"

His uncle swore and spat again. "Dammit, if any man has a right to feel wronged, it's you, boy, and I know it. Your wife cheats on you and walks, and then some foreign hood uses you as a pawn. You got a right to feel lower than a rattlesnake. But you don't have any right to lay down and die. Get that face repaired and then go after that girl before it's too late."

Blake turned his head to look at his uncle again, and his eyes were frosty. "What makes you think I want a woman who won't accept me until a surgeon's knife has transformed me into a socially acceptable pretty boy?"

Thad flushed, a dark, ruddy red. "I thought your daddy was the stubbornest mule on two feet, but you got him beat a mile." Thad twisted in the saddle to get a better look at Blake. "Did it ever occur to you that you might scare the hell out of a good woman with two eyes in her head? I swear to God, when I look at you straight on, you almost scare the hell out of me."

"I've never known you to turn coward before, Uncle," Blake said, tossing Thad's words back at him in that cool, dark voice.

"What is it you want? You want her to love you, ugly puss and all? Well, let me tell you something. That only happens in fairy tales. She'll find someone else and leave you sitting high and dry." Thad's eyes left Blake's; the leonine head turned to scan the prairie. "They say pride makes a cold bedfellow, but he don't make such a fine daytime companion, either." Thad scowled as if the landscape displeased him, but Blake knew that wasn't what had earned his displeasure. It was Thad's own admission, after forty years, that he'd made a mistake.

"And you ought to know about pride, Thad. My father's been dead for five years. Why don't you ask Mother to marry you?"

It was a blunt statement designed to throw Thad off the subject of Blake's infirmity. It succeeded. Thad moved his heavy body in the saddle, and those gray brows came together. "Because I'm not gonna ask till I get some sign from her that she's agreeable to the idea."

"Maybe she's waiting for some sign from you that you care about her," Blake said equably. "After all, you're the one who went off to the city and found yourself another woman to marry."

"Damned fool that I was."

"Of all the men in the world, you should know what it feels like to lose a woman you want. Why are you encouraging me to take Drew's woman away from him?"

Thad opened his mouth to say something, then clamped it shut again. "Never mind why I think what I think. That woman's right for you, son. She's the most right woman I've seen in a long time. She sets on that roan of hers like a piece of smoke, light and easy but sticky as glue."

"That makes her an excellent candidate to be my wife?" As Thad shook his head in disgust, Blake continued to study his uncle. "When did you see her ride?"

Thad's color rose again. "I was curious to see if she was good or crazy, this woman who took your daughter riding when she should have been home in bed."

"Doing a little spying? You amaze me, Uncle."

"Doesn't do any good to just look unless you're willing to act. I happen to be a man who likes to get things done."

"As long as they're done your way."

Thad sighed and lifted his reins. "I'm done jawing with you, boy. Ain't no use talking to a thickheaded mule like you. You're probably right. You couldn't get that woman, anyway. Drew's got the edge on you, seeing her every day at school—"

"Uncle." Blake's voice stopped Thad before he could ride away. "You owe the school some money. You are going to pay it, aren't you?"

"I always pay my debts, boy." His mouth twisted in an ironic lift. "I've been paying them for years." He stared at Blake, his eyes bright with wisdom . . . and regret. "Looks to me like you're gonna be doing the same thing."

He rode away down the slight hill, leaving Blake to stare after him. When he was younger, he hadn't recognized his uncle's hit-and-run technique. He did now. Thad had never studied a word of psychology, but he used several basic techniques. The old man knew there was nothing that set Blake's mind working faster than to throw out a challenge and walk away.

It wouldn't work this time. He wasn't going to compete with Drew for Jamie. She had a right to choose her own destiny . . . just as he had a right to choose his.

But even as he made that decision, the remembered feel of her lips, soft and pliant and seeking under his, made his body come to life with a now familiar ache.

Blake shifted in the saddle, feeling uncomfortable, as if his uncle had put a burr under him physically as well as mentally. Was there any parallel between his uncle's situation and his? He didn't see it. Forty years ago his uncle and his mother had been seeing each other, and they had talked of marriage. But one night there had been a misunderstanding and crossed signals. Ruth had thought Thad planned to pick her up and take her home from a church social; Thad had assumed she was going home with her parents. Stranded at the church with no way home, she'd accepted a ride from Thad's brother.

The next night, Thad, as angry as a bull in full charge and as blind and stone headed, had gone to her house and accused her of using his own brother to make him jealous. Ruth had denied his charges, calmly at first. Then her own anger had got the better of her, and she had allowed that she'd be crazy to marry a pigheaded fool like him who couldn't see past his nose. He'd gone to Chicago, found a woman who, unfortunately for Ruth, had fallen deeply in love with him. He'd married her too quickly, too thoughtlessly, and brought her back to Rock Falls. A year later, Ruth and John, Blake's father, had been married.

Blake shook his head. He couldn't solve Thad's problems; he had enough of his own to keep him busy.

He just hoped Drew didn't expect him to be his best man at the wedding. For there would be a wedding. Jamie Gordon was the kind of woman a man wanted to make his partner, for now, forever.

The pain rose again. Muttering a word under his breath, Blake touched the reins against Storm's neck and turned him prettily at the top of the hill to head for home.

THE NEXT WEDNESDAY EVENING, Tiki banged on Jamie's apartment door, said she was coming in, came in, tossed her sweater on the couch and wrinkled her nose. "I came to tell you your sub did okay in school today. This place smells like a massage parlor. Have you been using that medicinal rub for aching muscles again? You rodeo riders ought to buy shares in that company and get a little of your money back. Did you finally go to the doctor?"

"Yes. He said I'd sprained my thigh."

"Women sprain their ankles, not thighs."

"Don't tell me, tell the doctor. I have come to the conclusion that with George, all things are possible."

"Ah, yes, George. We can't blame George because you went out riding last night, can we?"

"No," Jamie said, her expression rueful. "Much as *we* might like to, we can't."

Tiki eyed Jamie. She was stretched out on the couch, a pillow under her head, a blanket over her leg, perspiration beading on her brow. "Been soaking in a hot tub, I see."

"Yes. That plus a day spent taking muscle relaxants, plus the miracle rub, and I'm still hurting. Did you take the rented bunny suit back to Sioux Falls?"

Tiki nodded. "Last night."

Jamie shook her head. "I don't think I'll ever be able to face another Easter."

"Easter?"

"All those cute little rabbits . . . and ducks."

Tiki sat down in a chair opposite Jamie, laid her head back and closed her eyes. "You didn't happen to see Blake last night, did you?"

"You're beginning to sound like Pauline Brighton."

Tiki lifted her head and looked at Jamie. "Who's Pauline Brighton?"

"A journalist who wants to do a story on Blake."

"But Blake, being Blake, refused."

"How did you know?"

"Blake is the kind of a man you just know about. No tricks, no pretenses. Straightforward. Self-contained. Solid. Right is right, and wrong is wrong. Lord, I wish I were right for him." Jamie put her head back again and closed her eyes, a dreamy half smile on her lips. "I'd sure like to have him come and tuck his boots under my bed for one night."

Jamie was extremely glad Tiki had her eyes closed. Her reaction to those words was almost physical. Imagining Blake with his hands threaded through Tiki's red hair, leaning over her, his marred face softened with sensual need, his body warm and naked, made her sting with an ache of her own.

"This is the age of equality. Maybe you should tell him how you feel." That sounded much crisper than she'd intended it to. Why was she saying these things to her friend?

"This may be the age of equality, but it isn't the age of stupidity. If Blake were interested in me even the tiniest bit, he would have picked up on it the night of the carnival. I paid eight bucks for the four kisses he gave me, but it was worth every penny."

"I must have missed a kiss sometime during the evening."

Tiki's eyes came open. Unmoving, she gazed at Jamie. "You were counting?"

"I was just curious."

"A lot of good it did me. Every time he just smiled that half smile at me and offered his mouth, as if he were helping me open a can of soup. But the minute you get in trouble, he rushes to your side. He captures George, extracts you from the pool and takes you home. And you're not going to tell me a darned thing about it."

"That's because there's nothing to tell. He brought me home, told me he thought I'd done something to my thigh and warned me not to ride for a week—"

"A warning you promptly disregarded because of his daughter—and ended up having to stay home a day from school. Honestly, Jamie, you're an intelligent lady, but sometimes you're not very bright."

"There was nothing I could do. I had to go."

"Yes, I suppose you did."

Jamie closed her eyes. She could see a man riding slowly over the horizon, dark, splendid, alone. All day, as she'd lain on the couch, the memory of him had haunted her. The sound of his voice echoed in her ears, but most of all, she remembered his smile. That rare, wonderful smile that held the subtlest hint of sexuality.... She would never again be able to look at a sunset without thinking of him.

"Well, if you want my opinion, Blake was right. You should have stayed off that horse for a week—"

"Yes, you should have," a low voice said from the doorway.

The husky, masculine tones that had echoed through her head were there in her apartment. And so was Blake.

Tiki, her restless energy suddenly restored, jumped up from the chair. Jamie tugged the edge of her robe and pulled it around underneath the belt.

"I did knock, but no one answered. Too much feminine chatter." Blake's eyes went to Jamie. "Jenny told me you weren't in school today, and I came to see how you were, but since you have company—"

"I'm just leaving." Tiki was comic in her rush to pick up her jacket and her purse.

"Don't go," Jamie said quickly, really wishing she wouldn't.

"I'm sorry. I must. I have ... papers to correct...." She looked at Blake. "Stacks and stacks of papers. You know how it is. A teacher's work is never done." Another brilliant smile.

Jamie swore that if Tiki flashed those white teeth one more time and uttered one more lie about how much work she had to do, she'd find the strength to get up off the couch and hit her.

"I'll see you at school tomorrow," Tiki said, heading for the door. "If you're feeling better, that is. Bye." And she was gone.

Blake turned slightly to watch Tiki close the door behind her. When he turned back to Jamie, he was smiling. "Another smart teacher. They do seem to be... proliferating in this part of the world."

"The state department of education will be so glad you approve. Would you like to sit down?"

"Would you like me to sit down?"

No tricks, no pretenses. Straightforward. Honest. Right is right, and wrong is wrong. Looking up into his eyes, she said, "Yes. I would."

She could have been wrong, but she thought she detected a slight softening in his expression. In fact, he looked... concerned. An irrational irritation arose. She wasn't Jenny.

He didn't sit down. Instead he walked around the couch and headed for the bathroom. A minute later a cold cloth was run gently over her perspiring face, then laid on her brow. She struggled, trying to dredge up a bit of the irritation she'd felt a second ago, but she couldn't do it. His thoughtfulness was as therapeutic as the cool moistness of the cloth. How had he known what she needed?

She looked up into those fathomless green eyes. "Some ice water helps, too," he said. "Mind if I make myself at home in your kitchen?"

"Please feel free."

He brought her a glass of water so cold that it was already beaded with moisture when he carried it in on the little tray. She drank it thirstily and then leaned back.

"How's Jenny?"

"Worried about you. She was torn between wanting me to stay and finding out how you were. I convinced her you

would see to it that I returned safely home. She's starting
to come around."

"I'm glad she's feeling more secure."

"You know, of course, that what you did for her yesterday meant a great deal to her. She hasn't stopped talking
about it. I may have a rodeo fanatic on my hands."

"Does that worry you?"

"No, not if you continue as her trainer." At the impli-
cation of a long-term relationship among the three of
them, her throat went dry. She took another sip of the cool
water and handed him the glass. Why did the room seem
filled with endless quiet?

He pulled the coffee table closer to the couch and set the
glass where she could reach it, considerate of her without
having to think about it.

Without having to think about it. Gentleness, consideration, caring were inbred in him, as much a part of him
as his head of black hair.

"I came to tell you how sorry I am that you're hurting
because of what you did for Jenny. If there was some way
I could make it up to you, I would." His voice was quiet,
but the intensity was there.

"You're under no obligation to me. I took Jenny riding
because I wanted to."

"And you don't believe in breaking promises to children."

His gentleness made her uncomfortable. "I honestly
didn't think I was this bad."

"You've been to the doctor?"

"He's said I have a sprained thigh and I'll get over it. Easy
for him to say." She tried a light laugh and moved on her
side to see him better, wincing from her effort. The cloth
he'd replaced on her head fell to the floor, but before she
could retrieve it he was there, picking it up and putting it

back on her head. He leaned over her, close, so close with that impassive, maimed face, and she was swept by such a wave of longing for him that she closed her eyes.

"I'll be going now." His voice was block hard, as frozen as the Arctic Sea, such a contrast to his warm tone of a moment ago that her nerves jumped with shock.

She opened her eyes. Straight as an iron rod, he stood beside the couch, gazing down at her with winter in his face. Instantly she knew what had happened. He'd misinterpreted her closed eyes. He'd thought she couldn't stand the sight of him. He was going to leave her, walk away from her a second time, not knowing the truth. Her body warm with temper, she reached out blindly. By some miracle, he was still close enough for her to grasp his hand.

"Wait a minute."

He went still, gazing at her with that austere face, but she was too furious to be intimidated. There was warmth in his grip. Warmth . . . and acceptance. Heartened, she said, "Stop making unflattering guesses about what I'm thinking." Her eyes flashed up at him. "If you want to know what's going through my mind, ask me."

In the silence she could hear herself breathe. If Blake was breathing, if he felt any emotion at all, she could see no evidence of it.

"What are you thinking?"

He sounded as if he didn't care, as if he were asking just to be polite. Losing a little of her steam now, and wishing she'd let him walk out the door, Jamie faltered and loosened her grip on his hand. "I can't tell you."

"I wonder why." The look on his face told her what he thought of her prevarication.

She flashed defiant eyes up at him. "Because it's X-rated."

He didn't react. He just seemed to be . . . absorbing it. "Now who's being kind?"

"I'm not being kind. I'm telling you the truth. Your face doesn't bother me, at least not the way you think it does. It only bothers me because you wear it like a badge—a . . . a Keep Out sign."

His pupils flared with reaction, darkening, deepening, pulling her inside those layers of green. Dear God, what was she doing? Why didn't he just go before she disgraced herself more than she already had by making it utterly clear that she liked him far too much?

He was silent, totally unmoving. Yet there was a subtle change in him, a change that made her breathing seem to falter.

"May I sit down beside you?"

Afraid to trust her voice, she nodded.

"Have I misjudged you so much?"

He smelled so good, felt so good . . . looked so good. Her throat seemed dry, her palms moist. "Yes. You have."

"Show me," he said softly. "Show me how much." There was nothing, absolutely nothing in his face to encourage her . . . but there was nothing to discourage her, either. Slowly, slowly, she raised her hands to his face.

With infinite care she cupped his jaw, then brushed her fingertips lightly over his cheeks, moving over the smooth cheek and the scarred cheek, exploring the difference in texture. He didn't move or draw back, but his eyes darkened. When she'd explored his face, she held his head and began to draw his mouth down to hers. "Kiss me, Blake," she murmured.

"You can't mean that."

"You . . . don't want to."

She looked drawn, hurt. The last thing in the world he wanted to do was hurt her. Yet he would. If he didn't kiss her, he would hurt her, but if he yielded to the temptation of that inviting mouth, he would hurt her far more. "You don't know what you're doing... what you're setting in motion."

"The world. I'm setting the world in motion. It's been still far too long."

There was nothing in his face that told her what he was going to do, nothing to prepare her for the sudden, swift lowering of his head, the covering of her mouth with his. She wasn't ready for his kiss, and yet she was. Far too ready.

His mouth was a shock and a revelation. How could a mouth that looked so firm be so velvety soft? The lean hardness of his body was no surprise, nor was the strength of his fingers cupped around her cheeks, but his mouth... oh, his mouth. This was not the teasing brush of lips he'd subjected her to the night of the fair, nor a mocking taking of what he wanted the way he had the first time he'd kissed her. This kiss held a world of surprising suppleness, of pliant, sensual seduction. This kiss held knowledge of her and a perfect willingness to act on that knowledge. The need for him expanded tenfold, centering deep within, exploding and building and building.

"Jamie." He murmured her name against her skin, his breath warm against her cheek. "What do you want me to do?"

What did she want him to do? Envelop her like the ocean, enclose her like the dark, surround her with his hard body. She wanted him to kiss her again, banish her doubts and fears with that pliant, demanding mouth. Never in her life had she felt this way. "I want you—" she hesitated, feeling as though she were teetering at the top of a high, swaying bridge "—to touch me."

"Where?"

The soft question might have been a summer breeze caressing her face. "Here." She took his lean, wonderful fingers and cupped them around her throat, at the pulsing vein that was the source of her life, her hand over his. "And—" she hesitated, looking into her eyes "—here." The feel of his fingertips against the soft, vulnerable beginnings of her breasts gave her a soaring elation, as if she'd moved from that swaying bridge to the edge of a cliff.

Blake groaned her name again in protest, a mutter of sensual torture. But the dark glow of his eyes matched the euphoric delight she was feeling, and directed by a primitive need inside her, she urged his hand lower until he was cupping her breast in the curve of his palm.

Unable to stop himself, he leaned over and took her lips again, moving over her mouth in a counterpoint to the lovely friction his fingers were creating against her nipple. She slipped her hands around his waist and up under his vest, testing the feel of his muscled back covered by the cotton shirt. She ached to touch his bare skin the same way he was touching hers.

"Smooth and soft and satiny and . . . what's this?"

He'd found the tiny mole on the side of her breast, the one she'd carried since she was born.

"Even imperfection is perfect on you," he said, and brushed his lips lightly over the star-shaped beauty mark. Then, as if he'd just understood his own words, he straightened, and his mouth twisted in that mocking smile she disliked. "Beautiful on the outside and on the inside, as well. Too beautiful and too kind to turn away the beast."

"You are not a beast."

"Perhaps not, but you bring to mind very . . . primitive thoughts, thoughts of picking you up and carrying you into your bedroom, making love with you until dawn."

Even while he said the evocative words, he had withdrawn his hands and retreated into formality, sitting up and putting distance between them. That half beautiful, half scarred face might have been a bizarre mask for all the emotion it revealed.

Her mind whispered that it was all part of his defense, but her pride cried out that it didn't matter what his reason, he'd as good as admitted his interest in her was sexual, nothing more. And she had encouraged him. She'd asked him to kiss her, to touch her. She'd invited his lovemaking, but now he was calling a halt to it . . . and to everything else.

She lifted sparkling eyes to him, her hand at the neck of her robe pulling the edges together. "I was told you were a brave man, but your courage seems to be limited in its scope."

As her words registered, a dark and dangerous flame flickered in those green eyes. "And you, Ms. Gordon, have more guts than sense. You think because you've prodded the beast once and he didn't turn on you, you're safe." He stood up and walked to the door. His fingers on the knob, he turned. "You're entirely too trusting. The time may yet come when I'll surprise you. And if it does . . . I'm not sure you'll like what you see."

NEVER HAD THURSDAY AND Friday of a school week passed by so slowly. The hours at school dragged, and her nights were haunted by things she wished she hadn't said to Blake. She shouldn't have called him a coward. He was anything but. She should have accepted his rejection gracefully and not lashed out at him. That wasn't fair.

When Friday night arrived and she'd grown weary of trying to decide whether to go to Blake and apologize,

Drew sauntered into her room and asked her to go out to dinner with him the next evening.

Was it a minor case of insanity? Or was it the hurt Blake had dealt her that made her accept? She didn't know. She only knew that anything would be better than staying home and thinking about Blake.

Saturday night arrived at something far faster than the speed of light, and she was seated in the car beside Drew, waiting for the blessed distraction that would take her thoughts from Blake.

Was there that much distraction in the world? She didn't think so. Locked in the seat next to his cousin, she remembered the way Blake had looked just before he'd kissed her, the way he'd looked when he was touching her... and the austere expression on his face when he'd stood at the door.

What experience had Blake had that made him want to hide behind his scarred face? For that was what he was doing, whether he realized it or not. He was afraid to feel, afraid to love.

Love. What did she know about that elusive emotion? She'd thought she was in love with a man once, but it had been an illusion. She liked men, as friends. But what she felt for Blake Lindstrom wasn't friendship. It was something much... stronger.

Knowing that, she had grasped desperately at diversion and accepted Drew's invitation. Now here she was raising false expectations in Drew's mind. Her attempts to make things better had made things worse. How had she become a pawn between the two men? And how could she extricate herself without hurting one or the other of them?

During dinner with Drew, she called on every scrap of discipline she had to concentrate on him. He was more than willing to carry the burden of the conversation, telling her about one of his brighter students and how the "practical-minded" creature had wanted to know how people had existed before television. The lack of other more basic facilities, like pure drinking water and indoor bathrooms, hadn't occurred to him.

Jamie tried to nod in the right places and show genuine interest, but it was hard. She kept thinking of Blake, wondering where he was, what he was doing . . . and if he was thinking of her.

"The key to the whole thing was to tell them it was like *Little House on the Prairie*—without Michael Landon. Then they seemed to catch on— Are you going to make me talk nonstop through the entire evening, or are you going to tell me what's been rolling around inside that beautiful head of yours?"

Caught, she raised startled blue eyes to his. She should have known she couldn't fool Drew. His years of training as a teacher had made him too watchful, too perceptive.

"It's nothing, Drew. Just . . . a problem I was trying to work out."

"This problem wouldn't by any chance be wrapped in a package six feet three inches tall that's thirty-one years old, would it?"

She looked over his shoulder to the tiny floor where couples were dancing. "The music is nice, isn't it? They're a good group."

Drew leaned back in his chair. "Okay, we'll play it your way. You can be silent and enigmatic for now. You look far too gorgeous tonight. I haven't the heart to badger you. But later . . ."

"The wine is excellent. Would you pour me another glass?"

ABOUT MIDNIGHT Blake gave up trying to sleep. Lifting himself out of the small cot and groaning softly at the pain in his cramped muscles, he walked to the window. Illuminated by the moonlight, the ranch shone like a smooth silver plain. A breeze had risen as the night cooled, and the air from the open window sang past his face, stinging his cheeks, bringing him to life.

In the moonlight the land lay flat and dark, filled with cattle and promise. The memories of his land and of Jenny, all bound up together, had kept him alive during his captivity. A year ago, after his wife had left him, he'd stood here and promised himself that he would make the ranch his life. He would spend every waking moment developing it, building the herd and eventually, adding land. It would be both his obsession and his refuge. And his legacy to his daughter.

Yet tonight it failed to shelter and protect him as it had before. There were pictures in his mind, pictures of his cousin, Drew, bending to Jamie, fitting his lips to hers, even as Blake had a few nights ago.

Blake muttered a curse. He wasn't an infatuated boy to stare into the night and moon over a woman. If Jamie Gordon kissed or made love with Drew, it was nothing to him. To her, Blake wasn't a man; he was a character in a fairy tale, a glorified, wounded hero.

Unbidden, the feel of her mouth on his washed over him, coupled with the pliancy of her body. Beyond all logic or reason, he wanted her. Wanted her with a desperation he didn't understand.

Why had he walked into the airport and gazed immediately into that face, which made all the others unimportant? Why had he talked to her, watched her smile, held her and, not just once but several times, taken that soft, yielding mouth with his?

Cursing again under his breath, he stood for a moment longer, looking out over the silvery landscape, fighting to banish the mental picture of Jamie and Drew entwined. He stood for a moment longer, his body aching. Then, knowing there was nothing else he could do, he went back to his cot beside the bed of the sleeping child, and collapsed on it.

6

DURING THE EARLY MORNING HOURS, a rainstorm blew up. The random crackle of lightning and banging of thunder suited Jamie, the chaotic bursts of sound matching her state of mind.

"When I'm worried and I can't sleep, I count my mistakes instead of sheep."

Mistake number one. Going to the airport with Drew.

Mistake number two. Watching Blake Lindstrom greet his daughter.

Mistake number three. Going to dinner at the ranch with Drew.

Mistake number four. Walking out to the stable with Blake, kissing him.

Mistake number five. Kissing him at the parent-teacher fair.

Mistake number six. Asking him to stay in her apartment when he was ready to leave.

Mistake number seven. Letting him leave when she wanted him to stay.

Mistake number eight. Going out to dinner with Drew.

Why had she gone out with him? Because she'd wanted to forget. And instead she'd learned just how far down the road she'd gone toward . . . what?

Toward becoming a one-man woman.

Friday afternoon, when she'd accepted Drew's invitation, she hadn't known. But by Saturday night, when Drew had walked her up the stairs to her door, pulled her close and tried to kiss her, she'd known then. She'd turned her head and avoided his mouth, resisting him. He'd been hurt and angry, and she'd said nothing to ease his pain. How could she? How could she explain that she hadn't known until that exact moment that the only mouth she wanted on hers was Blake's, the only face she wanted to see was his, the only touch she wanted were those supple, lean, far too knowledgeable hands . . .

The sun began to lighten her room, and with the memory of Blake still filling her mind, Jamie dozed.

When she awoke it was nearly noon. After a breakfast-lunch of juice and coffee, which was all her stomach would tolerate, she showered, got dressed and forced herself to wade into the stack of work that waited for her. Shortly after two o'clock in the afternoon, just as she was racing down the homestretch through the first set of math papers, Mrs. Fairfax, her landlady, appeared at Jamie's apartment door. Her prize roses needed a drink. Would Jamie please help her turn the eaves spout so that the next time it rained, which would be tonight, according to the forecast, her flowers could get a drink of water?

Knowing that the next set of papers would take forever, the fairy tales she'd had her pupils read and rewrite in their own words in preparation for the clay modeling project, Jamie dismissed all thoughts of getting her work done before evening, tossed her pen on the table and told Mrs. Fairfax she'd be glad to help.

Eaves spouts were low on Jamie's list of things she'd most like to tussle with. She'd helped her mother wrestle with the heavy wooden storm windows on their Iowa farmhouse, and that was the extent of her expertise in house maintenance. She understood about eaves spouts, though; they did double duty. They were the mysterious funnels through which rainwater was collected and stored in cisterns, and they diverted rainwater from the soil around the foundation to keep the house from becoming a rival to the Leaning Tower of Pisa. Excess rain had never been a problem in eastern South Dakota, but this was a rare spring. They'd had an ample amount of moisture in April, and still the rains hadn't stopped. There was some talk about sandbagging along the Missouri River.

Yet with all this precipitation, Mrs. Fairfax's roses hadn't gotten their share because they grew under the overhanging roof, and the eaves spout was turned to drain into the cistern.

Dressed in a T-shirt and jeans, Jamie was glad she'd had the sense to put on her old sneakers. The mud around the cistern was rich and black, and she was forced to stand in it to reach the spout. It extended like a mail chute at shoulder height and could be moved to pour its river of water into the ground cistern or the flower bed that bordered the house. They'd had so much rain the night before that the cistern was full to the brim. But the protected earth around the roses looked bone dry.

The bottom part of the eaves spout should have been moveable—and wasn't. Jamie tugged and twisted, trying to get the elbow pipe to move inside the upright one. It wouldn't budge. Jamie continued to strain and tug, but nothing moved, and she was afraid that if she twisted it harder, it would snap. Even to Jamie's inexperienced eyes, it was obvious that the spout had been in its present position all winter, long enough to rust into place, probably permanently.

"I'm sorry," Jamie said to the currant-plump woman who stood safely on the lawn away from the mud and the rusty water pouring from the elbow joint Jamie had managed to loosen enough for water to leak out. "I don't think I can do it without a tool of some kind."

"Oh, dear. I suppose I can water them with well water. But it just isn't the same. The poor things don't like the taste of all that iron...."

Jamie looked into Mrs. Fairfax's sad eyes and knew she wouldn't be able to return to her own work with a clear conscience until her landlady's flowers got their drink of water. "Let me see if I can find some tools to do the job."

There was only one family in the area she knew well enough to ask for help. She thought of telephoning the Lindstrom ranch first, then decided that was foolish. She would simply hop in the car, drive out to the ranch and collect whatever tool Blake suggested for the job.

On the way there, Jamie found the gravel softened by the rainfall treacherous at best and deadly at worst. Fortunately, the condition of the road demanded that she keep her mind on her driving, not on her destination. When she arrived at the ranch and knocked on the door, it was Blake who opened it. Had he, in the country way, looked out the window to see who had driven into the yard and known who it was before he opened the door? If he had, it might explain his lack of surprise.

His eyes went over her as if they enjoyed the sight of her. Or did she think that because she was starved for the sight of him?

"If you're looking for Drew, he isn't here."

Shaken, she said the first, most inane thing that came into her head. "I wouldn't be here at all if it weren't for Mrs. Fairfax's roses."

The corners of his mouth turned up slightly. "I've never been grateful to a rose before."

Chemistry. It was instant chemistry, what he did to her when he relaxed his mouth that tiny bit. His quiet smile sent a zinging pain to the pit of her stomach. "She wants to water them with rainwater, and I can't turn the eaves spout. I need a wrench about this big. . . ." She shaped a luncheon-plate-sized circle with the fingers of two hands that weren't quite steady.

"And probably some oil, too, I would guess," he said.

"Oil?" She sounded like an idiot. Maybe that was because she felt like one.

"To loosen the rusted joint. This sounds like quite a project. Would you like a helping hand to come along with the wrench?"

He said it in the coolest, most blasé way possible. How could she refuse? "If I'm not taking you away from something here."

"We're finished with dinner." Again that slight half smile. "We eat at noon, if you remember."

"Yes. I remember." She remembered too much. He looked so good standing on the porch step clad in dark dress pants and a white silk shirt and tie. He'd been dressed just as formally the day he'd walked into the airport, but his face had been etched with fatigue then. Now there was something else in his expression, a composed watchfulness, a wariness. What was he thinking? As usual, she didn't know. His face was smooth, his hair neatly combed. "You'd better change." She brushed a hand down her thigh in a deprecatory gesture; traces of mud clung to her jeans and sneakers. "It's not exactly the neatest place in the world to work."

For an instant his eyes flickered over her. Then they came up to her own. "I'll bear that in mind. Would you like to come in while you wait?"

"No, my shoes are too muddy. I'll wait in the car."

She walked back down the steps, her shoulders hunched. *Well, what did you expect? Did you expect him to greet you with open arms?*

Just for a moment he almost had. For one beautiful moment he'd looked glad to see her. And he'd smiled.

SHE LOOKED TIRED, Blake thought as he climbed the stairs to change his clothes. But it wasn't the right kind of tired. It wasn't the sensual lethargy a woman wears when she's been made love to by a man. She looked genuinely exhausted and strung out, edgy as a cat. It was as if something had been bothering her and she'd lain awake most of the night thinking about it. What kind of thoughts put those dark circles under her eyes and brought the tension to her mouth?

Drew had called and said he wouldn't be coming to the family dinner today, and Blake had assumed Jamie was with him. The thought had eaten into him all morning. He hadn't blamed Jamie. He'd merely cursed himself for a fool. She'd handed him an open invitation, one he'd thrown back into her face. If she'd turned to his cousin, how could he blame her for that?

But suppose she hadn't stayed the night with Drew? Suppose Drew had bowed out of the family dinner because he'd been irritated by his failure to make love to Jamie and hadn't wanted to betray his state of mind with an unguarded look or word? It was an intriguing thought, one Blake would never have had if he hadn't seen Jamie this afternoon.

Dressed in his old jeans and his work boots, he went downstairs and out to the machine shed. When he returned with the wrenches and oil, she was standing by the side of the car, her face turned into the breeze, her hair blowing away from her head, looking toward the stable.

"How's Jenny?" she asked.

"A little better. We're trying to get her weaned away from me for short periods of time. Mother managed to bribe her with a Disney movie matinee to give me a few moments of peace."

"And I've destroyed them. I shouldn't have come. Why don't you just give me the tools and—"

He caught her elbow. "It's all right. I don't mind."

She stood looking up at him, caught, her body alive with anticipation. "Would...would you like to ride in with me?" Without blinking she added, "I'll be coming back out this way again to check on my horse, so it won't be any trouble to run you back home."

She made it seem so logical, so sensible that he didn't see how he could refuse. "If you're sure you don't mind."

"I don't," she said.

"Fine."

Riding in the car beside her, he liked the way she drove. She seemed to know instinctively how fast she could go on the loose gravel and still maintain control. Did she make love that way, controlling the agony, prolonging the ecstasy until the last possible moment? It was an idiotic thought to have, and yet he couldn't seem to keep from remembering how exciting her body had felt under his hands. Her hands were long-fingered on the wheel, capable, but on his face they had been infinitely gentle. And she'd touched his scar without distaste or disgust. She'd looked curious, the way she might look if she were touching more of his body.

The physical reaction to his own thoughts was instant. He was glad the road required her strict attention. Instead of submerging his desire for her, he let his eyes wander over her, over the slimness of her thighs in the oft-washed denim, the slender perfection of her arms extended to hold the steering wheel, the cameo smoothness of her cheek and jaw. She was a young, beautiful woman, and he wanted her. More than that, he wanted to immerse himself in what she was, light and happiness . . . and freedom.

Jamie knew he was looking at her. She could feel the tension in his body, the change in his breathing, a change that elicited a response deep within her. She searched her mind for something to say and could think of nothing. She hadn't bargained for this. She had thought she would talk to him for a few minutes, collect the tools and leave. Yet the silent tension in the car seemed to bring her alive. Whatever Blake was thinking, he wasn't immune to her. He was as aware of her as she was of him.

Mrs. Fairfax was at Jamie's side the moment she emerged from the car. "Oh, how nice. You've brought Blake along to help. It's so good to have a man one can turn to."

Blake's eyes went to the older lady's doting countenance, and he smiled a genuine smile that teased only slightly. "It's nice to be appreciated, ma'am. In these days of feminism, we men sometimes feel . . . nonessential."

"That's nonsense. Women will always need men, just as men always need women," she said matter-of-factly, then realized what she'd said and turned a charming shade of pink.

Jamie took pity on her. To Blake she said, "The eaves spout is on the east side of the house. I hope you took your vitamins this morning. It's turning out to be a recalcitrant beast. . . ."

Blake's face changed ever so slightly, and Jamie's voice died away. Then, determination in her face, the glitter of the sun in her eyes, she looked up at him. "Exactly like some men I know."

Mrs. Fairfax gave a little gasp, but Blake's mouth softened and relaxed. Softly, for Jamie's ears alone, he murmured, "You have a wide experience with recalcitrant men?"

"It's getting wider by the minute," she muttered back to him.

"Poor lady." He sounded extremely unsympathetic.

He asked for the keys to open the trunk. When he'd collected everything he needed, Jamie turned to lead the way to the eaves spout, Mrs. Fairfax trailing behind Blake.

In the shadow of the overhang, Blake cast a caustic glance over the offending joint, shaking his head. "I'm not sure I can free it without twisting or damaging it."

"It doesn't matter," Mrs. Fairfax said stoutly. "If I have to buy a new section of pipe, I'll need the old one out of there, anyway."

"I'll see what I can do."

Blake laid a thin stream of oil around the seam of the joined pipes, set the oilcan down and tried a turn of the spout. It didn't move. "Come around here and hang on to this downspout," he directed Jamie. "Maybe I can get more leverage on the other section."

Jamie took a firm grip on the pipe, but Blake twisted it out of her hands.

"I can't use a wrench; it will crush the pipe. Let's try it again."

Jamie recognized the look on Blake's face. It was the look of men the world over, pitting themselves against metal. She hoped the roses would appreciate his efforts.

The pipe gave a little; water oozed form the seam and ran down Jamie's pant leg. "Lovely," she said in an ironic tone.

Blake looked up, smile lines at the corners of his eyes. "We must be getting somewhere."

His determination, combined with a muttered curse, made metal grind against metal. The pipe gave an inch. "Okay. Hang on again."

Mrs. Fairfax stood on the lawn making fluttering noises and starting sentences like, "I really hadn't meant for anybody to go to all this trouble."

Blake's eyes met Jamie's over the top of the pipe, and his lips twitched. Jamie smiled back, sharing his amused tolerance...and for that one blazing moment, it was as if they were one mind shared by two bodies.

Then the moment vanished. The muscles in Blake's arms and shoulders strained, the pipe gave ... and a stream of muddy water gushed out and poured down his shirtfront.

"Oh, dear. Oh, dear. Goodness me." Like a fluttery bird, Mrs. Fairfax chirped the bad news.

Jamie stared at Blake. He looked...strange. A whole procession of emotions flickered across that normally impassive face: consternation, annoyance, surprise, and then, his eyes locking on hers, ruefulness, as if he should have expected this from an escapade with her. "You and water are a lethal combination."

It was said so dryly that Jamie laughed with relief. The iceman thaweth. "I'm sorry, really I am. But you look so...startled."

"I'm glad you find me amusing." She expected the mockery, but it wasn't there. He wasn't angry, either. There was a warmth in his voice that had been missing before, a warmth matched by the gleam in his eyes. Warmth and below, a wonderful body that was streaked with muddy water from the second button of his blue chambray shirt to well below his belt buckle.

Jamie averted her eyes. "You'd better come up to my apartment and get cleaned up."

"I'm not sure if I dare get that close to you in a place where you have access to an unlimited water supply."

Chuckling, she leaned against the house.

"Really, Jamie." Mrs. Fairfax was all stiff disapproval. "I hardly think it's a laughing matter. Blake, I do apologize—"

"No problem. I'll wash."

"Well, you must come inside and let me—"

"Miss Gordon has already offered, and since she enticed me into this job, she should be the one to clean me up, don't you think?"

JAMIE SAID LATER, when she stood in the bathroom laying out towels and soap, "When she saw you were really going to come up here, Mrs. Fairfax didn't know whether to be shocked at me or angry at you."

"Actually, she knew if she protested she'd be contradicting her own liberal views. After all, she'd just said that men needed women and women needed men." His face was as dispassionate as ever but . . . watchful. "Does she object to your having a man in your apartment?"

There was a subtle quality of challenge in his tone, but she ignored it and said lightly, as if it were nothing more than a casual question from a friend, "I don't know. I don't put it to the test very often."

"I wonder why." Blake was watching her with that speculative look in his eyes.

"I wonder, too." She sounded as if she really did. "Look, don't you think you ought to take those off and let me run them through the washer and dryer? Otherwise what will your mother think?"

"What will she think if I do?"

Jamie ignored his lazy drawl, but she couldn't ignore the heat in her face. "If you don't tell her, I won't. You can wear my robe while your clothes are washing."

"That serviceable garment I saw you in the other evening?"

"One and the same. It may lack aesthetic value, but it will cover you. It's hanging behind the door."

She waited, wondering if he were the kind of man who wouldn't consider donning a woman's garment.

"I'll see if it fits."

His smile was slow, lazy. Jamie, her throat tight, nodded and closed the door.

She was humming tunelessly as she walked into her little kitchen. What did she have to serve him for a light supper? Nothing alcoholic of interest; she and Tiki had drunk all the wine the other night. There was always iced tea, of course.

She fixed the tall glasses and garnished them with a slice of lemon. She heard the water running in the shower and knew it would be a little time yet before Blake was finished. Sandwiches, she thought. Nothing special. Tuna or slices of chicken breast that she'd bought at the deli.

She decided on the chicken. That called for toasted bread and mayonnaise and lettuce and dill pickles. She scurried around the kitchen, hoping to have everything laid out before he came back.

"Are you expecting company for dinner?"

Her muted humming had obliterated the pad of his bare feet across her floor to the kitchen. He had his muddy clothes in his hands...and a towel around his hips. Nothing more.

Had she thought he was lacking in self-confidence? How wrong she'd been. No male could have been more lazily blasé about his lack of attire than Blake Lindstrom. Long, lean legs, dark curling hair, crisp little whorls of it everywhere. That's what Blake was made of. Her throat went dry; her stomach muscles tightened. Trying to avert her eyes, and discovering two well-shaped tanned male feet in her vision, she reached for the clothes. Here was a man who, despite his disfigured face, exuded sexuality with every breath.

Breathe, move, think, she told her body. The message came back. *Mission impossible.*

"You decided not to wear my robe." She took the clothes and was thankful that the washer was on the other side of the kitchen. She was able to turn her back to him as she tossed them in, added the detergent. The sweet, clean smell of the soap drifted up to her nose. Would she ever be able to breathe or swallow normally again?

"You have to give me an A for effort, Ms. Gordon." The lazy drawl was to remind her of her teacher status. "I tried. I got one arm in. If I'd had the other, I would have ripped it down the back."

She should have known his shoulders were too wide to fit into her robe. Trying not to think of wide shoulders, wide, bare, muscular shoulders that somehow looked even more impressive than they did when he wore a shirt, she closed the lid of the machine and punched the button, knowing as she did so that her last line of defense was gone. This time there would be no bundle of clothes to stop her eyes from going wherever they wanted to go. She leaned her hip against the washing machine and turned to look at him, ruthlessly disciplining her eyes to stay trained on his face and using every ounce of her energy to look as casual as he did. "Nice of you to be so careful of my clothing. I've fixed iced tea and sandwiches, a sort of consolation prize for the ordeal you've been through. Won't you sit down?" She tried a nonchalant wave of her hand in the direction of her kitchen set. The chairs were chrome and wicker, but the top of the table was glass. Glass. She would choose glass. Standing in the furniture store, she hadn't envisioned half-naked men tucking their well-shaped, muscled legs under it.

With a slight smile on his face that meant anything—or nothing—he moved to seat himself. She turned away and picked up the tray. Carefully, keeping her eyes on the tinkling ice cubes in the glass of tea, she set his in front of him. "Would you like sugar?"

"No, thank you."

"A sandwich?"

"Yes, please." He was so polite, so cool, but underneath the table the towel strained along the line of his flat stomach and lay loosely along one lean thigh, barely covering it. She dragged her eyes upward . . . and discovered he'd caught her looking in all the wrong places. Frozen, unable to tear her eyes away from his, she waited for some sign that he'd noticed her errant gaze. As calmly and as coolly as if he were formally dressed and dining at an afternoon tea party in a rose garden, he picked up his glass and drank.

Her face burning, she longed for just a tiny bit of his controlled calm. That was what it was. It wasn't indifference. He was as aware of her as she was of him. That Viking blood might be ancient history, but it was there, beating in the veins of this twentieth-century man, a man who'd learned to control all his impulses.

What would it be like to watch him lose that control? What would it be like to be the woman whose touch made him tremble?

She tried the tea and was able to take a swallow without choking. A sandwich was beyond her. He watched her replace the plate without taking one and said, "You're not eating."

"I'm not as hungry as I thought I was."

"Or as sophisticated, either, perhaps."

"Sophisticated?" Her eyes raised to his, blue depths probing green. As usual, they betrayed nothing.

"Are you finding it hard to—" a pause "—look at me?"

Nerves taut, she set her tea down on the table, glass clicking against glass. "I've never found it difficult to . . . look at you."

She sat still, waiting for his reaction. There was none, no change of expression in his face, no answering flare in his eyes. Despite the kisses, he simply was not interested in her. He was, in as polite a way as possible, saying no.

Feeling embarrassed for him and for herself, she got up from her chair, the glass in her hand the excuse she needed to go to the sink. She turned her back to him, set her glass on the counter and braced herself against it with both hands.

Blake sat watching the slender woman bowed over the counter. Now that he was alone with her in her apartment, where intimacy and lovemaking were possible for the first time between them, she'd kept her distance, politely but nevertheless firmly. She was trying to let him down easily, but she was killing him with kindness—didn't she see that?

He didn't want her to be kind. He wanted her to be torn apart by the sight of him. And what had he provoked in Jamie? He'd provoked her charity. Her sympathy. Her determination to, above everything else, treat him with kindness.

"Would you like help with the dishes?"

"No."

"Thank you for the sandwich. You'll let me know when my clothes are ready?"

At the cool tone in his voice, she turned. "Yes, of course."

For a long silent moment they looked at each other, each waiting, each believing the other was uncomfortable and wanted to leave. At last Blake got up from his chair and went into the other room, his bare legs dark under the whiteness of the towel, his straight back discouraging any attempt she might have made to continue the conversation.

The washer stopped, and she transferred his clothes to the dryer, her fingers fumbling just a little with his dark bikini shorts, thankful that his well-worn jeans wouldn't take too terribly long to dry. She stayed in the kitchen, cleaning out a cupboard she'd meant to get at for ages, but as she took the spices and boxes out, wiped the shelves and replaced the things neatly, she worked automatically. Her mind and her body were tuned in to the other room.

He hadn't turned on the television. He'd evidently found a magazine. Once in a while she could hear the pages turn. She rattled the dishes and tried to hum again, but the melody seemed to escape her.

After a long interval she pulled his clothes from the dryer, trying to ignore the feel of the soft cloth of his underwear. She folded his jeans, laid his socks and shorts on top and covered them with his shirt.

He'd evidently heard the machine stop. He came to the door, and when she turned with his clothes in her hands, he was leaning against the frame.

"You didn't have to fold them."

She should have been prepared for the sight of his lean, male, almost-nude body this time, but she wasn't. It struck her with the force of a tidal wave. "I know." She forced herself to walk across the kitchen to where he stood and hand them to him, her senses alive, clamoring to touch the drying hair, to taste the hollow of his throat. . . .

Dark, green, unreadable—maddeningly unreadable— eyes looked back at her. "Thank you. I appreciate it."

"You're welcome."

He stood looking at her for a moment longer, and she forced herself to return his gaze without looking away. But when he turned and went into the bathroom, she leaned back against the door, her knees trembling as if she'd been in a war. And she had. The trouble was, she was fighting herself. And losing.

He came out in what seemed like no time at all, fully dressed except for his boots, which he'd left outside the door next to her sneakers.

"Thank you for your hospitality."

So polite, so formal. "You're welcome."

"I guess I'm ready, if you are."

She looked at him blankly, then remembered. She had to take him home. "Yes, of course."

Telling herself she should be sorry this interlude was going to be prolonged, and irrationally glad that she could be with him a few more minutes, she went into the bedroom, slipped her feet into moccasins, grabbed her riding boots and purse and followed him out the door.

The ride to the ranch was uncomfortable. He made no attempt at polite conversation, and neither did she. It seemed a long twenty miles. When it was over and Blake was climbing out of the car, she pulled the keys from the ignition to open the trunk for him to take out his tools, wishing that she'd never driven out to the ranch to ask for Blake's help. They'd worked together and laughed together, but he was more remote than he'd ever been.

Outside the car, while Jamie was standing waiting for the inevitable goodbye, the breeze blew her hair up around her head, baring her nape. She reached up to smooth it down, and for the first time she saw something in Blake's eyes, something she had looked for since the night of her escapade with George. Then it was gone. Was it a trick of the light? Or had he really looked at her...and desired her?

"Thank you for your help," she said to him, her voice cool and polite.

"Anytime." He was equally cool, equally correct.

She got into the car and circled to drive back down the road.

Blake stood watching her, a curse escaping his lips, directed at his inability to break down the barrier between them.

IT RAINED MONDAY AFTERNOON and drizzled Tuesday. It looked little better Wednesday, but Jamie had missed too many practice sessions with Strawberry already, including the one she could have had Sunday if she hadn't been caught in an altercation with Mrs. Fairfax's drainpipe, and with Blake. She had to take Strawberry out after school and run the kinks out of her, rain or no rain.

It was a slow, dripping rainfall, the kind that seemed to seep into the bones. The alfalfa smelled wet, laden with nutrients, the earth muddy, the air moist. Under the leaden sky Jamie guided her horse around the first barrel, not really trying for speed, working more to limber up the mare's legs and her own body. The slicker crackled against the saddle, and Strawberry's hooves made a sucking sound in the mud. Every single brain cell told her she shouldn't be out here in the rain. But there was no guarantee that her first rodeo competition wouldn't be held in a downpour, and this was good practice for both of them.

So she went round and round the three barrels set at the corners of a triangle, trying to work up her speed, trying to overcome the feeling of laxity, practicing with her mind as well as her body, visualizing speed, thinking speed.

Jamie rounded the last barrel, and her hat fell off her head to dangle by the strings around her throat. Her wet hair streamed across her face. Half-blinded, she yanked her hair back from her face and used the ends of the reins on Strawberry's flank to urge the horse into a galloping run.

When they crossed the line, Jamie knew her time had been good despite the mud. She'd beaten the elements, she and Strawberry. Tossing her hat to the sky, she lifted her face to the rain and laughed out loud at its drizzling wetness, and when she caught her hat and lowered her head to replace it, she discovered Blake mounted on Storm, sitting there waiting for her.

He, too, had a slicker on, but unlike her he wore a hood. Shadowing his face as it did, the hood gave him a dark, saturnine appearance. "Only a damned fool laughs at the rain."

She bowed her head in ironic acknowledgment. "Did you ride all the way out here to tell me that?"

"I rode over here because I wanted to talk to you."

He hadn't meant to sound like a heavy-handed father. He'd only known that watching her take the horse at steadily faster speeds around those steel barrels over the rain-soaked slippery earth made his heart come into his throat. One slip of those graceful legs and Strawberry could go over, dumping Jamie down on the barrel, or falling on her and wedging her between a half ton of horseflesh and that unyielding steel. He'd seen the scars on her ankles from the brushes she'd had with those barrels.

Why did she have to ride in the rodeo, compete, take risks? He didn't want her to take risks. He wanted her to stay safe. Safe from harm.

That was idiotic. Why should he be concerned about her safety? Unless...he was beginning to care for her. Too much.

She lifted a hand and pushed back a soaked strand of hair that clung to her cheek. "What did you want to talk about?"

7

BLAKE DIDN'T WANT TO TALK to Jamie there in the pouring rain. He wanted to turn and ride away from her, prove to himself that the sudden, blinding revelation he'd had while he sat there and watched her jockey her horse around those barrels in the rain was nothing more than his overactive imagination. He wasn't falling in love with her.

He struggled to direct his mind back to the problem that had brought him riding out to see her. She looked anxious for him to say whatever he had on his mind and leave.

"I've come to warn you."

"Warn me?"

He had her interest now. The smooth cameo face, beaded with rain, was turned up to his, and her mouth was moist and wet.

Knowing he shouldn't, he urged his horse closer. In the smoky-gray light of a setting sun hidden behind the clouds, her skin had the opalescence of pearl. "Jenny's completed her clay sculpture."

"Sculpture?" She knew what he meant, but it didn't make any sense. Why had he come out in the driving rain to talk to her about Jenny's schoolwork?

"The sculpture showing a scene from the fairy tale she's studying."

He didn't name the fairy tale; he didn't have to. She knew exactly which one Jenny was working on. "Of course."

He gave her a strange, rather oblique look. "I understand they discussed the project with the substitute teacher, the day you were gone."

"Yes, they did. The woman left notes of what she'd said and the pupils' response, and I was pleased. She did exactly as I'd asked, stressed that the figures should be familiar and have some basis in reality. The magic of fairy tales is derived from the pleasure of reading about what seem to be real people."

He rode closer, so close that their legs were almost touching. She could see his face in minute detail. Long, black lashes dropped over Blake's eyes. The lashes were damp and spiky, thick and incredibly appealing. They wanted touching. "Yes, I understood that was your approach. Jenny has also said that there is to be an exposition this Friday, and that you plan to display the sculptures then. Is that correct?"

"Yes, that's true."

It wouldn't be an exposition. It would be an inquisition specially designed to torture the teachers, Tiki had muttered after the faculty meeting a month ago. Who in the world had ever heard of holding a show during the last days of school?

Drew, as smoothly as ever but ruffling Tiki's feathers, had explained, "Babe, in these political woods, you don't understand that our beloved principal Coachman has to do everything he can to convince this community to keep its school. And if appeasing the taxpayers means throwing the school open and showing all the children's work from the past year that's fit to be displayed, that's what he'll do."

Blake's words brought Jamie back to the present. "I want you to promise me that whatever...feelings you may have about Jenny's work, you won't ask her to withdraw it.

She's just beginning to show some signs of losing her morbid fear about me, and I don't want anything to upset her just now."

Jamie drew herself up in the saddle, conscious suddenly of the restless movements of her horse. Strawberry sensed the closeness of Blake's stallion. Every female in the vicinity seemed to be losing her sense of perspective. *Steady, girl. Let's both keep our heads. I don't know about your male, but mine believes I have the sense of a rabbit.*

Rivulets of water ran down her neck, and there was a curious ache in the region of her heart. What kind of teacher did he think she was? "Ask her to withdraw it? Why would I do that?"

"Give me your promise."

Her chin went a fraction higher. "There's no need to give you a promise about anything so elementary. Under no circumstances would I stop a child from exhibiting a piece of work just because it didn't meet the artistic standards of some small-minded adult." Her eyes flashed at him, pinpointing exactly who the small-minded adult was that she had in mind.

Unruffled by her jab, he said, "Then you agree that Jenny's work should be displayed, regardless of any personal feeling you might have about the project?"

"Of course I do." She was angry now. He'd insulted her, made her sound like an emotional two-year-old rather than a mature adult who understood the responsibility a teacher had to deal fairly with her students.

"Fine. I'm glad we agree. I just wanted you to know that under no circumstances do I want Jenny's sculpture withdrawn from display. She's been working on it for hours every night, and it's important to her. I don't want her to be hurt."

"I would never hurt her, certainly not in that way."

Under the slicker's hood, he dipped his head to her. "I'll count on you to keep your word."

At the expression on her face, he gave her a half-cynical smile, wheeled Storm and rode away from her.

IT GOT DARK rather quickly after that, with the grayness and the rain, and if that weren't discouraging enough, Jamie's concentration was destroyed. She stabled Strawberry a half hour after Blake had gone.

In the dark, damp, hay-filled barn, she wiped the horse down automatically, her mind on the face of Blake Lindstrom. What had he been thinking of, to come riding out in the rain and accuse her of withdrawing Jenny's sculpture willy-nilly on some emotional whim? Why would she think she'd consider doing such a thing?

She went over Strawberry with the currycomb, taking the tangles out of her long mane. The man had taken leave of his senses—that was the only explanation she had. Now if he would just take leave of *her* senses . . .

Why couldn't she get him out of her mind? He seemed permanently lodged there, the scent of him, the feel of him, the look of him. She hardly saw the scar anymore. It was a part of him, like the shape of his arms with the curl of muscle riding under the skin, or the way he sat on a horse, as supple as a willow.

BLAKE'S EASE OF MOVEMENT struck her again the next morning as he walked down the school hall toward her, carrying a big cardboard box, Jenny's sculpture project. One or two other mothers had brought their children to school in the car rather than risk having a clay creation meet with the demolition crew disguised as fellow bus passengers. Child after child had come in beaming, cradling his or her project as if it were a newborn kitten. The cardboard box tops that most had used as sturdy transport proliferated everywhere in Jamie's classroom, along the shelf under the window, at the counter around the sink and on the reading table.

Tiki had come in to admire the cornucopia of creativity. Snow White, a little tipsy but resplendent in white net snipped from a grandmother's high school formal, was next to Rose Red, equally tipsy, equally early-fifties elegant. Cinderella, one clay shoe tied to her wrist, waltzed around her coach, which had just been turned back into a clay pumpkin with indentations far too crooked ever to be found in nature.

Now, standing in the hall for her inevitable stint of morning duty with Tiki, Jamie watched with something like pleasurable shock as Blake came closer. She hadn't thought he would be the one to carry Jenny's project carefully through the big door and down the hall, but when she looked at him, hatless, his dark hair tossed about his head in careless beauty by the morning breeze, his shirt rolled up above the elbows as if he'd already been out working on the ranch, he looked controlled and incredibly earthy.

Was there anything more attractive than a man caught in the act of being a father? Right now, she didn't think so. Blake had a look of grave interest on his face, looking down at his daughter. Jenny skipped along beside him, chattering her delight.

"Miss Gordon. Daddy brought Beauty and the Beast in to school for me."

"That was nice of him, Jenny. I can't wait to see what you've done." To her disappointment, the box was covered. She glanced upward . . . and found Blake looking at her with that same intent look he'd given her yesterday. "Have your dad set it on the reading table."

Blake turned to follow Jenny, and when they disappeared into the classroom, Tiki turned mischievous eyes up to Jamie. "Is it my imagination, or was the atmosphere a little thick there for a moment? What's going on between you two? Have you been holding out on me?"

"No. It's . . . nothing."

Which was true, as far as it went. Probably Tiki would have believed her, if Blake hadn't returned to her side and said in a soft voice, "I'd like a word with you, if I may."

Tiki's red-gold eyebrows went skyward. "No problem. I'll take a walk down the hall."

Jamie faced Blake and found she was nervous. Her throat was dry, her palms wet. Now what?

"I just wanted to remind you that we have an agreement."

"An agreement?"

"About Jenny's sculpture."

Her nervousness vanished, detonated by her anger. "You're spending a lot of time and excess energy worrying about something that isn't going to happen."

"I have your word on that?"

"I don't need to give you my word." She tried to sound cool, professional. She was very much afraid she sounded scathing. It was a natural defense and the only one she had to cover up the hurt.

"I want your word."

"You have it." She clipped out each syllable as if she were chipping them out of an ice-cube tray.

He dipped his head, and when he looked at her again his gaze traveled over her hair, combed up into a disciplined topknot, her smoothly prim powder blue dress with the A-line skirt, her sensible flat shoes made for running around the playground. He didn't move a muscle. It had to be the tricky lighting in the hall that gave his eyes a suspicious gleam of . . . what? Admiration, amusement . . . possession. Male possession. Green lightning. She felt the sizzle to her sensibly shod toes.

"Have a good day, Ms. Gordon."

As agile as a tiger, he turned and sauntered down the hall, his boots making an unfamiliar sound on the tiled floor.

Now why should she get that flicker of fear in the pit of her stomach just because he'd looked at her and wished her a good day?

"What was that all about? Or do I dare ask?" Tiki reappeared at her elbow, her eyes alive with curiosity.

"It was nothing, really. He had this idiotic idea that I'm going to keep Jenny from exhibiting her project at the open house because it isn't good enough. I tried to explain that this wasn't an art contest, but . . ."

Tiki frowned, staring after Blake, who was opening the front door and disappearing through it. She swung her head back to Jamie. "Maybe we ought to check out that sculpture."

"I'm sure it can't be that bad."

"Let's go have a look, shall we?"

THE DAY WAS LONG, infinitely long. By three-thirty, when the last child went out the door, Jamie's headache raged on, unabated by the four aspirin she'd taken over the past six hours. Utterly grateful to stop pretending the world hadn't collapsed, she sank down at her desk in the empty classroom and buried her head in her hands.

"I'm going to take a picture of you, call it Teacher at the End of the Day and enlarge it. There will be bills passed instantly all over the country to raise our salaries."

Drew strolled in and closed the door behind him, studying her face while he walked. "You'd be better off if you'd sit down and have a good cry, but let's have a look at the thing first, shall we?"

"You've heard?"

"I've heard of nothing else all day long. Where is this Rodinesque masterpiece?"

"At the back of the reading table."

"Ah, yes. I see it." Drew stuffed his hands in his pockets and, as if stalking a cobra, strolled toward the table laden with clay figures.

He stood there for a long moment, looking. When he raised his eyes to Jamie's, they were certainly sympathetic. "Crude, but effective. The spirit is certainly there even if it lacks a little in technique. We Vikings seem to be harboring a budding artiste in our midst. Who would ever have thought the little beggar had such talent?"

"Who, indeed?" Jamie's lips lifted in a self-mocking smile.

"I must say, the child has an eye for detail. The eyes, the mouth, the hair..." Drew paused, perusing. "All yours, Jamie. Beauty, reclining on her couch. Even the legs complete in net stockings are undeniably yours. And leaning against the tree, proffering a rose to you, we have Blake, in as complete detail. Of course, there's no missing him. He's remarkably easy to spot with that half beautiful, half horrible face of his. Jenny's caught that arrogant way he holds his head, as if the world were all his."

Drew looked up, and from across the width of the room, she felt the force of his gaze. "There won't be a doubt in the world about who either of these two people are. The entire community will know exactly who Jenny sees as her Beauty and Beast. You won't, of course, allow this to be shown."

She was so tired, so very tired. And her head hurt, had been hurting for what seemed like a hundred years. "I gave Blake my promise I wouldn't withdraw it."

Drew swiftly crossed the room and, clamping his hands on her shoulders, pulled her up out of the chair. "You gave him your promise? How could you possibly do that?"

"I didn't know what it was . . . never guessed. He came out to talk to me yesterday, and he asked me to give my word—"

"Before you'd seen it?" Drew's face grew red with anger while he muttered a clipped curse, followed by Blake's name. "My God, I knew he was ruthless. But this . . . this borders on cruelty." She shook her head, and Drew's fingers tightened on her shoulders. "Listen to me. It's bad enough the whole school has heard about it. You can't possibly exhibit it. You'll be committing career suicide."

"Blake doesn't know that. He was thinking of Jenny. She's his first concern."

"The hell she is. You're his concern, whether he knows it or not, playing the gallant, making a play for you in front of your landlady—" At the look in her eyes, he said in a savage tone, "You wonder how I know? Half the town knows, and the other half will know it tomorrow. Jamie, for God's sake, you can't put the sculpture on display—"

"I can't stop it," she whispered. "I gave my word."

Drew stared at her for a moment and then dropped his arms. "You're a first-year teacher here. Coachman doesn't want a breath of scandal to touch this school. He'll eat you alive, and when he's finished, he won't offer you a contract for next year. Worse, he won't give you a recommendation."

"I . . . have to take that chance."

Drew swore, a sharp, incisive curse. "Damn that cousin of mine. He thinks he's the only one in the world, he and his pride. I'm going out to the ranch and talk to him."

That brought her head up. "Don't you say a word to him, Drew, not a word. I won't have this be the cause of more trouble between the two of you."

His fists were knotted at his sides. "You expect me to stand by and watch him destroy you? You expect too damned much!"

"I'm not going to be . . . destroyed. Perhaps Coachman won't think anything of it, and neither will the community."

"You've been spending too much time reading fairy tales. You're beginning to believe them. Jamie, listen to me—"

"No, you listen to me. If you do anything, anything to interfere, I'll no longer consider you my friend."

Drew studied her, his face a mask of disapproving amazement. "I think you mean that."

"I do. Believe me, I do."

"You'll lose your job . . . and you won't have a prayer of getting another without a recommendation."

"Then maybe I'll have to go on the rodeo circuit to make a living."

"That's not a living. That's cruel and unusual punishment."

"Promise me you won't interfere."

He drew back from her a little to examine her face more closely. "He's gotten to you, hasn't he? You'd rather lose your job than break your word to him."

Her chin came up. "Why is it men think they're the only ones with a sense of honor?"

He was silent for a moment, studying her strained face. "If I talked to him, explained that your job was at stake..."

"The end result would be the same. Jenny would be terribly hurt. And there would be talk she wouldn't understand."

He swore again in a soft, savage voice and released her. "My God. He doesn't deserve your consideration."

THAT EVENING, when she was alone in her apartment, her determination faltered. Despite her efforts to put Drew's words out of her mind, she couldn't. She liked teaching; she wanted to continue. And teaching left summers free to ride the rodeo circuit. If she could talk to Blake, persuade him to have Jenny alter the figures slightly, that might be a reasonable solution.

On Friday morning, an hour before she had to be at school, she rose to a damp grayness. She hoped to make it out to the ranch before it started to rain, but she didn't. It was drizzling when she drove into the ranch yard.

Blake was there, in the south corral. There were men with him—his foreman, Jed, and two other wranglers she didn't know. She did recognize the bulky body of Thad wrapped in a yellow slicker.

She'd worn her old boots, but she tried to watch her step as she walked through the ranch yard. The mist enclosed her in a blanket of fog and moisture. Hard to see anything but mud. A rivulet ran through patches of clay-soft ground from the barn on a meandering path toward the machine shed. Never had they had so much rain in South Dakota. The rivers and the streams were bloated beyond a level anyone had ever seen.

She went to the corral and propped one foot on the lower rail. The men were working at full tilt, branding, using a table to hold the calves steady in the rain. One bawling calf was about to be freed from his prison. A cowboy grabbed a calf, took a hoof in the stomach, let out a curse, looked up, saw her and gulped. "You got company, Blake."

One yellow-slickered back parted company from the rest; Blake turned.

For a moment she thought he didn't recognize her. Perhaps he didn't. She had on her own rain gear, a conservative beige coat with a sheltering hood that she wore to school when they had rare days like this.

Blake, his slicker half-open, displaying a tantalizing glimpse of his lean body, moved to the other side of the rail and stood looking at her. "I should have known I'd be seeing you today."

"Should you? How?"

"It's such a nice day."

Despite herself she smiled, and amazingly, so did he. "A noted authority on such things once told me only damned fools laugh at the rain."

He smiled quietly. "What did he know?"

She faced him head-on, her eyes catching his and holding them, refusing to let him look away. "You knew a lot more than I did, at the time, it seems. You might have told me the truth about Jenny's sculpture."

"I might have, if you hadn't been so quick to think I was usurping your authority."

"So instead you gave me enough rope to hang myself."

Now it was his eyes that clung to hers. "Something like that."

She swallowed, wishing she didn't have to stretch that little bit to see him over the top corral rail. He was able to see her with no problem at all. She gritted her teeth.

"I wonder if you'd consider having Jenny change her sculpture slightly."

The smile faded; his expression cooled. "I wouldn't consider having her change it at all . . . even slightly."

"There are things you don't understand."

His eyes flashed green fire. "I think I understand. You've come out here to tell me you've reconsidered and you can't possibly keep your word."

Her voice low, she said, "I just don't want to expose you—or Jenny—to any more embarrassment."

"And what about you, Ms. Gordon? What about your embarrassment?"

"I'm not embarrassed. It's just that—"

"Just what?" He stood staring at her, water dripping from the yellow hood. "You would rather not have your name linked with mine?"

The heavy irony in his voice acted like a fuse to dynamite. She went hot with anger. She was furious with him for lifting her spirits with that rare smile at the beginning and then dashing her so cruelly with his cold anger, and furious with herself because she cared so much about how he felt and what he thought. "You're asking for it, cowboy."

Stepping to the corral and wrapping her arms around a post, she hooked a boot on top of the second rung and stood up. That brought her skyward enough to look down at him—and put her within kissing distance. Teetering over the top board, she grabbed his wet slicker and pulled him toward her.

He was too startled to resist, and she was too angry to stop. Deliberately she pulled the hood off his head, wrapped his chin in her fingers, got her other arm as far around those yellow-slickered shoulders as she could and brought his lips to hers.

He'd never been kissed by a woman with anger on her mind instead of sex, and he found it incredibly exciting. Her mouth was rain soft, feminine, its dark secrets promising other sweeter secrets in the soft recesses of her body. Desire seared through him.

Blake's warm mouth and his willingness to take what she gave, whether it was offered in anger or in passion, softened her fury. His cheeks were rain wet and cool, his lips dry and willing. More than willing. He was warming to his task nicely when she put her hands up to push him away. She was too late. Far too late.

Blake reached around and slid his hands under her coat, brought her up closer and locked the upper half of her body to his, mentally consigning to the depths the fence that kept him from taking the sweet weight of her hips against his. Every nerve, every muscle, every bone cried out in a fever. He'd kissed this lady one too many times. He wanted more than kissing. He wanted to feel her soft flesh under his, her breasts as pliant as her mouth. He wanted to absorb the warmth and heat of her into his body, his brain, his soul.

Behind him, one cowboy hooted while another gave a long, piercing wolf whistle. More than happy to turn away from the monotony of work, they gave all their attention to Blake and Jamie.

Jamie waited for Blake to loosen his hold on her. Instead his fingers tightened. There was wild recklessness rising in Blake—she could feel it in every bone in her body. Yet his desire for her didn't frighten her. His tongue probing restlessly in her mouth filled her with a heady sense of power. Here, in the rain, half-suspended on a corral, he wanted her. But the power flowed both ways. He was tearing down her last defense against him. He smelled of earth and rain, and the storms inside him were flowing free, setting off answering disturbances in her.

Under her coat, his hand wrapped around her rib cage, and the top of his fingers nudged the soft underside of her breast. Rocked with the need to feel his hand touching her without the restriction of clothes, she breathed in deeply and pulled away.

Though she was released from his kiss, the heated need she was feeling echoed from the depths of those green eyes looking at her from under a hat that dripped water.

"If we weren't in such a damn public place—"

She felt as if she couldn't breathe. "Blake, I—"

"I'll come to you...later. We'll have dinner together. Go home and wait for me."

"Blake—"

He bent toward her and kissed away her last attempt to stave off the inevitable. Seconds later he lifted his mouth an inch away from hers as if he could hardly drag himself away. "Eight o'clock," he murmured huskily. "Wait for me." His hands tightened on her. "Promise me, Jamie."

Dazed, she nodded. He released her body but held her hand to steady her as she backed down off the corral fence.

Being earthbound didn't help. Her body was still humming with sensual need. He reached over the fence and ran a finger down her nose. "See you later, honey."

"Yes," she said, a drop of rain falling on her lips, making her aware of their swollen warmth as she turned to walk to her car.

Blake stood watching as she started the car and circled to leave the yard. Then, as he turned, a whack on his back nearly made him lose his balance.

"I told you she was the woman for you, didn't I, boy?" said Thad gleefully. "She's got nerve. Even if she is a schoolteacher, I like her style. Which is more than I can say for you. Haven't you got any more gumption than that? Snag her. Don't let her off the hook."

Blake turned to his uncle, knowing the other man hadn't heard anything. He believed only what he saw, that Blake had let Jamie walk away from him. His mouth curved. The urge to return measure for measure of his uncle's needling made him say, "I never was a good fisherman."

"Fisherman, hell. Time's a wastin'. You aren't getting any younger. We need a boy in the family to carry on the name. And that lady has the brains to let the rein out . . . just enough . . . to get you roped and hog-tied before you know what's happened to you. What are you standing around here for? Go after her."

Blake smiled. "I've got cattle to brand."

Thad scowled at him, not understanding that mocking, amused lift of the mouth. "You'll be sorry. I know damn well, as sure as I'm standing here soaked down to my shorts, you'll be a sorry man."

"I wonder," Blake murmured.

THAT EVENING he was in his room when his uncle came up the stairs with the force of a bull elephant at mating time. Thad was talking before he stepped across the threshold. "Your mother tells me you're not eating with us tonight, and I'd like to know why in tarnation you aren't coming to the table like a civilized man—"

Unable to resist seeing the expression on Thad's face, Blake turned to face his uncle. "What's the matter? Is my tie crooked?"

The spectacle of Thad rendered speechless brought another smile to Blake's lips.

"Well," the older man said at last, in a long explosion of sound. "Well, well, well. Fancy silk shirt, string tie, suit pants, new boots—and if my nose doesn't deceive me, you took a long, hot shower and chased your deodorant with some fancy, store-bought cologne." The gleam flickered like the start of a fire in Thad's eyes. "Are you going somewhere?"

"Yes, you might say I'm going somewhere."

"With someone?"

Blake picked up a brush, bent to look in the mirror and ran it over his dark hair, frowning critically at his reflection. "You might say that."

"Now see here, boy. You tell me I *might* say this and I *might* say that, and you admit nothing. Are you going to see that little schoolteacher or aren't you?"

Blake laid the brush on the dresser, in the mood to give as good as he got. "What would you say if I told you no, I'm going to a meeting on artificial insemination for my cattle?"

"I'd say you were a damned fool."

Blake turned his back on Thad and walked to the bed, where his gray suit jacket lay with the hanger still in it. He flipped the hanger out and shrugged into the suit coat, turned to tug the bottom of the jacket and give himself a last cursory look in the mirror. "Then that makes you a bigger fool, doesn't it? Because you're going to go back downstairs and put your feet under the table that belongs to a woman you've loved for forty years—but you're too damned proud and stubborn to admit it."

Thad flushed a dark red. "Are you going to a meeting?"

"Are you going to do something about my mother?"

Thad stood for a moment, his face a slightly less vivid shade of pink. He stared at Blake and then began to chuckle. "By God, I always said you'd amount to something sooner or later. Any man that can get the best of me without lifting a finger—"

"What about you? When are you going to 'amount to something'? It's already too late to be sooner for you, and if it gets much later, Mother will find another man to soothe her injured pride just like she did the first time, and you'll lose her again."

Thad's fists balled at his sides. "Who would she find? Charlie Matlock, who can't fall asleep unless he drinks a fifth of whiskey? Monroe Farley, who's so much in debt he'll never get out? Bah!"

"There's a simple way to keep her from turning to another man. Go downstairs and declare yourself."

Thad was quiet for a long minute. Blake thrust a hand in his pocket and waited, watching the man he'd alternately loved and skirmished with all his life struggle with the forces of love and pride that were tearing Blake himself apart.

"Go on, Thad. Make Ruth your wife, and then perhaps you can forgive Drew for being born."

"Bah. That's all a bunch of poppycock."

Blake lifted an elegantly clad shoulder. "Is it?"

Thad lowered his head and stared at Blake. "You still haven't answered my question."

"You still haven't answered mine," Blake said pleasantly.

Thad muttered a curse under his breath. "If you aren't the stubbornest, proudest mule—"

"How could I be anything else, related to you? Why don't you set me a good example, Uncle? Go downstairs and propose to my mother."

"And if I do, will you—"

Blake shook his head. "I can only promise to dance at your wedding, nothing more."

Thad muttered another, slightly saltier word, was silent for a moment and then said, "I'll think about it."

BLAKE DESCENDED THE STAIRS and walked quietly into the den that was his domain. There was a computer on his desk, a small love seat with a tear on the seat cover that he'd never bothered to have fixed, a television set. Jenny was curled up on the side of the love seat where the cushion wasn't torn, staring at the television. At his entrance, she looked up at him as if he were an unwelcome intruder on her privacy, her eyes sliding over him, absorbing his unusually formal dress. The hurt she was trying desperately to hide shone from her like a beacon. She wasn't crying, but what he saw in her face affected Blake more strongly than tears. There was a stoic acceptance of pain, as if she'd learned the hardest lesson of childhood, that adults didn't always mean what they said.

"Hi," he said softly, going toward her.

"Hi." Her greeting was listless, and she immediately returned her attention to the television. It was a program of her favorite puppets, but Blake doubted if she could have told him what was going on.

He sank on the couch beside her and picked up her hand. There was no response from the small fingers. "I'm going out for a while this evening, Jenny."

"I know," she said without taking her eyes from the television, purposely ignoring him.

"I'm going to see Miss Gordon."

That brought Jenny's gaze away from the television to sweep over him in childlike disdain. She didn't say a word, but the message was in her eyes. Was that supposed to make her feel better?

For a moment Blake entertained thoughts of calling Jamie and telling her he'd been delayed, of staying with Jenny until she went to bed. But what would that solve? If she awoke and found him gone, she would trust him less than ever.

Frustrated, he let Jenny's unresponsive hand return to her lap and thrust a hand through his neatly brushed hair, casting about for the words to reassure his daughter.

He had none. And what was worse, Jenny's stoicism reminded him of his own pride and unwillingness to show any sign of weakness during his time of captivity. He'd hated having his life in someone else's control, he who had been in charge of a ranch and was used to giving orders, not taking them. Now Jenny was feeling the same thing. She had no control, and she was afraid.

It was all her imagination, of course. He was as close as the telephone on the desk. He'd left numbers with his mother about where he could be reached.

And then it struck him. Jenny didn't know that. He'd left the control with her grandmother. He had to put the ability to reach him at any time where it belonged: in Jenny's hands. But how could he do it without frightening her more than she already was?

Blake stared at the puppets on the screen, a famous troupe used to teach children letters and numbers. If he had a puppet to show Jenny how she could reach him anytime she wanted to . . .

Inspiration struck. He rose from the love seat, went to the desk and found a fine-point pen. He returned to his seat beside Jenny and with elaborate care turned his right hand over and began to draw a face on the tip of his index finger. He wasn't an artist, but by steadying one set of fingers against the other, he managed to create two eyes, a dotted nose and a smiling mouth. He even managed to draw two hair curls, one on each side.

Jenny turned her head away from the television. "What are you doing?"

"I'm making a picture of you."

Intrigued, Jenny forgot a small portion of her aloofness and unbent enough to ask, "Why are you putting it there?"

"To remind me that anytime I want to, I can find a phone and use my puppet Jenny to call my real Jenny." He wiggled his finger at her, and she smiled. "There's the puppet, Little Jenny." Blake paused and then said casually, "Would you like to have a puppet Dad?"

"Yes," Jenny said instantly, her eyes flashing up to his, not quite understanding, yet beginning to trust him again.

Blake picked up the finger that seemed small compared to his own and with careful concentration drew another face, this one with the mouth turned down and a few tufts of straight hair pulled over the forehead. "Looks just like me, doesn't it?"

Jenny smothered a giggle and wiggled the end of her finger. Blake was amazed to see how the little figure seemed to take on a life of its own. "Your mouth doesn't go like that. He isn't you."

"No?" Inwardly Blake winced. So much for his attempt at child psychology. "Who is he?"

"His name is Sam." Jenny wriggled her finger again, looking very pleased.

Determined, Blake tried again. "Okay, he's Sam. Anytime you want to talk to me, you take Sam to the phone and have him dial these numbers." He turned her palm over and wrote both Jamie's number and the number of the restaurant where he'd made reservations for dinner. When he finished, Jenny closed her fingers over the numbers as if she were preserving a treasure.

"So you see," Blake said, smiling at her, savoring her answering smile and the warmth that had replaced the look of hurt in her eyes, "I'm leaving Sam the secret agent here to watch out for you. And anytime you want to use him to call me, you can. All you have to do is dial the secret code." He tapped the knuckles of her bent fingers. "Meanwhile," he said, watching her, "the real Daddy needs a kiss."

"Can Sam really call you anytime?"

Blake didn't hesitate. "Anytime. All he has to do is take a walk over to the phone."

Jenny was silent for a moment longer, her eyes searching his as if she were hardly able to believe her good fortune.

"About that kiss . . ." he reminded her, his voice gentle.

With a choked cry and a reckless abandon that gave Blake a glimpse of the anxiety Jenny had locked up inside her, his daughter threw herself at him, locking her small arms around his neck. "I love you, Daddy."

"I love you, sweetie," he murmured, bringing his hand up to clasp her head, feeling the silken flow of her hair under his palm.

The girl lunged away from him and caught his hand. "Don't rub off Little Jenny."

"I wouldn't dream of it," Blake said, smiling down at his daughter, his heart overflowing with love.

"Sam wants to kiss her goodbye." Solemnly Jenny touched her finger to Blake's. Then she folded her fingers over her palm, enclosing the precious numbers. "Maybe you better go. Miss Gordon doesn't like people to be late. And the sooner you leave, the sooner I can call you."

Blake smiled. "Our reservations for dinner aren't until nine, so we won't be at the second number until then."

Jenny nodded solemnly. "I'll remember."

He stood up, and as Jenny's eyes shifted back to the television, he leaned over and kissed her on the head. "You be good and go to bed when you grandmother tells you to."

"Yes, Daddy," Jenny said, her eyes still on the television.

Blake, feeling better than he had in months, turned to leave her.

8

JAMIE WASN'T NERVOUS getting ready to go out with Blake, she was just having a run of unfortunate accidents. Spilling the bath powder all over the bathroom had been the harbinger, and from there it had gone from bad to worse. Pulling her hose on, she'd put her fingers through the delicate nylon and had to change them. The dress she wanted to wear was in the back corner of her closet. While she was searching for it, another blouse and skirt slithered off their hangers and fell to the floor. She fished out the dress she wanted and rehung the other garments, muttering a pithy word as she tossed the dress on the bed. A few minutes later, in front of the mirror in the bathroom, she concentrated carefully on applying her eyeliner. But her attention didn't help. She smudged it twice and had to remove it and apply fresh. By the time she was ready to shed her robe and put on her dress, her hands were shaking.

All right, so she was nervous. She'd made a tacit promise to Blake, and though she didn't regret it, she was aware that she had stepped into deep water. Now that she was away from him, reason reared its ugly head, riding in tandem with pride. Suppose he didn't really care for her? If he'd asked her to go out with him because he felt obligated after she'd made a fool of herself in front of his men . . . She shuddered at the thought and plucked a strapless bra from a drawer, the only one she could wear under the dress she'd chosen, a shimmery silk bronze tube held up with spaghetti straps and covered with a figure-hugging jacket. Beset by doubts, she put on the dress and slipped into strappy sandals with impossibly high heels. If nothing else, she wanted to be able to look Blake in the eye.

When her door buzzer went at ten minutes after eight, she was grateful for those few minutes of grace he'd given her. She had used them wisely, redoing her mouth and then heating water for a cup of herbal tea. It was while she was sipping it to soothe her nerves that he arrived.

Had she thought she couldn't look him in the eye? She could hardly tear her eyes away from him. He wore a light gray summer-weight wool suit that was Blake to the last thread, the jacket Western styled with V insets of velvety suede. Underneath he wore a matching suede vest that hugged his torso and a snowy-white shirt of silk. His boots were new, a slightly darker shade of gray than his jacket, the toes as shiny as ice. He smelled delicious.

While she was taking inventory, so was he, his eyes traveling over her slim shoulders, narrow waist, long legs encased in hose, slender feet perched on the high heels. She was as feminine as he was masculine, and his eyes told her he liked the difference. "You look lovely."

"Thank you. So do you."

He smiled at that, and though she knew he meant to relax her, that slow, lazy smile had just the opposite effect. A tingle descended her spine and centered in the low spot in her back. "Come in, won't you?" The invitation gave her an excuse to step back from him. "Would you like something to drink before we go? I was just having tea. I can brew another cup, or you can have something stronger if you like—" She turned away, playing hostess with a vengeance to escape those intently sensual green eyes, when an arm slipped around her waist from behind and caught her. She went still instantly, aware to her toes of the warmth and strength of that male body pressed against her back.

"Coward. Where's that woman who accosted me so boldly this afternoon?" The muttered, teasing words came to her ear on the rough velvet of his voice. "You were very brave when there was a fence between us. Maybe I should have torn those rails out and brought them along."

His humor gave her breathing space and the courage to push gently against him to gain her freedom. His hands left her body, his reluctance to let her go evident in the long, slow slide of his fingers from her rib cage. "The sight of you dragging six-foot sections of rail fence up the staircase would give Mrs. Fairfax something to think about, wouldn't it? Did you decide what you wanted to drink?"

His eyes moved over her face and settled on her mouth. "What were my choices?"

"Tea," she said quickly. "Coffee, orange juice, and—" her eyes flashed "—white wine. Isn't that a maiden-lady schoolteacher's proper menu of drinks?"

Blake's mouth quirked. "I was teasing you that day, you know."

"And I rose to the bait so beautifully."

"You don't really like Manhattans, do you?"

"I loathe them." It felt good, this exchange of honesty. He met her gaze with the same thoughtful smile of a minute ago, and she wondered if that was exactly what he'd had in mind. He looked as if he were in the mood for honesty. . . in all things. She turned away, deciding he was going to get tea whether he liked it or not. She wouldn't willingly put anything stronger in the hands of this man. He was more relaxed and charming than she'd ever seen him—and ten times as lethal to her peace of mind.

When she turned away from him again, he said, "Jamie."

His voice sounded strangely serious, no longer teasing. "Yes?"

"Jenny may be calling soon. I gave her your number. I'm sorry, but I—"

"You don't have to apologize. I understand. Do you like sugar in your tea or honey?"

He followed her out to the kitchen, aware as he hadn't been before that she was wearing her hair up. The sweet vulnerability of her nape with its tiny curls tore at him. He wanted to lean over and press his mouth to her warmth and smell her, taste her . . . until there was nothing left in the world but the feel of her soft, silky skin under his hands and the scent of her skin surrounding him.

Jamie led him out of the kitchen, every nerve in her body conscious of his tall, lean form behind her. She fixed his tea, leaving it unsweetened as he instructed and, avoiding his eyes, handed it to him. She invited him to sit down, but he shook his head and stayed where he was, one hip braced against the counter next to her phone. Taking her cue from him, she did the same thing, remaining a little way from him.

He was waiting for the phone to ring, she knew that, but the air of expectancy hanging between them had nothing to do with Jenny's calling. Blake looked casual enough, and he was talking easily, telling her about the television show Jenny had been watching when he left, but there was an undercurrent of unspoken communication between them.

Come closer, Jamie.

Not yet. Give me time. Please. . . .

A few minutes later, the phone rang. Blake lowered his cup to the counter and said, "May I?" Jamie nodded, watching his hand stretch out and pluck the phone from the wall receiver.

He was patient and kind with his daughter, letting her talk as long as she wanted to, answering her questions without a sign of irritation. When the conversation ended and he'd hung up the phone, he said, "I've promised her we'll be at the restaurant at nine. Perhaps we'd better go."

"NOT MANY WOMEN WOULD GO OUT with a man who has to orchestrate his time to accommodate his daughter," Blake told Jamie later. They were seated at a table in an old-fashioned Victorian restaurant with high corniced ceilings, snowy-white tablecloths and glittering chandeliers. The place had been built during the Gold Rush era, and its historic atmosphere had been lovingly preserved. Jamie had heard the food was excellent.

"You don't have to apologize to me," Jamie said quickly. "You know how I feel about Jenny."

"Yes," he said, watching her above the big silver menu the waiter had handed him. "I know how you feel about Jenny. But I don't know how you feel about anything else. Like sole, for instance. Do you like sole?" Again that devastating smile. "It goes well with white wine."

"In that case, I'd better try it," she said lightly, striving to take his teasing in the same vein that he gave it.

He ordered the sole Amandine for her and a surf-and-turf combination for himself. "Oh, yes, and we'll have white wine for the lady. I'll have a Manhattan up, please." His green eyes glinted with satisfaction as he looked at Jamie.

She ignored the gentle taunt and settled back in the comfortable chair. With Blake safely across the table from her, she could relax. Whatever else he might be, Blake was a wonderful escort even while he took care of his responsibilities to his daughter. Her heart thumped. The complete man, strong yet gentle and tender. She hadn't known such a man existed. She certainly hadn't guessed he lived behind the wintery eyes of the man who'd walked into the Sioux Falls airport and scooped his daughter into his arms all those weeks ago.

The publicity about him had died. When they had walked into the elegant dining room, a startled look or two had been thrown Blake's way, furtive, surprised appraisals of his scarred face. But no one seemed to recognize him. As for Blake, he'd ignored the curious glances and focused all his attention on her. While they waited for their food, he made conversation easily. She found herself savoring every word of his droll story about how a cow had turned on one of his hands and run the young man halfway across the pasture and over a fence.

Jenny's phone call came just after the food did. Without any sign of irritation, Blake rose from the table, telling Jamie to go ahead and eat her food while it was hot. His back to her, he strode to the phone. Without his presence across the table, she felt...let down. The dining room that had looked so lovely a moment ago lost its sheen, and she discovered she really wasn't hungry. She sipped her wine, waiting for him, knowing this was what her life would be like when Blake was no longer in it. Unless...unless he was beginning to feel about her the way she felt about him.

Before she'd eaten more than a few forkfuls of the tasty fish, Blake returned. The food suddenly tasted better and so did the wine. She drank a second glass and, by the time Blake had finished his meal, she was feeling extremely mellow.

Blake appeared to be as relaxed as she was. He smiled often at her, and every time he did she felt as if the alcoholic content in her blood doubled at an alarming rate. She was intoxicated on those smiles, lifted into a rarefied stratosphere by those smiles. . . .

They ordered coffee. As they sat sipping it, a small combo began to play. The trio of piano, bass and drums was doing a set of dreamy old-time ballads, the ones that invited slow, snuggled-close dancing. Jamie had expected Blake to ask her to dance and was disappointed when he didn't. She thought about telling him how remiss it was of him but she knew she wouldn't.

When her eyes drifted back from the floor, she found him looking at her. "No," he said softly. "Don't ask me to hold you close in a public place again. I'm tired of having an audience when I have you in my arms." At the startled look she gave him, he shook his head. "It's time we were going home."

He rose, pulled a bill from his pocket and tossed it on the table. Coming around to her chair, he cupped her elbow in his hand. She felt herself escorted, with a sense of urgency, through the carpeted hallway and out to the car.

The night air was like cool silk on her face. She settled into the car beside him, knowing she'd never felt like this before. She seemed to be melting into the darkness surrounding the car, into the night sky bright with a million stars, into the scent emanating from Blake's skin. . . .

At her door, dazed, she fumbled in her shoulder purse and found a hard, metallic object that seemed to be the right thing. She unlocked the door, stepped inside and turned on the light.

Just then the phone rang. Muttering a word under his breath, Blake lost a bit of his patience. He led Jamie to the couch and gently pushed her down into it.

She leaned her head back on the cushions, euphoria still running through her veins like a stream of mountain water, making her head light. She felt as if she were full of stars, each one of them a supernova exploding inside her. Something wonderful was going to happen, something that had to do with Blake's low voice, which she was hearing now....

His low voice stopped. There was silence in the apartment. She closed her eyes, waiting, waiting ... and his hands were lifting her.

She was in her own bed, her head resting on the pillows. Blake sat beside her, reaching for the lamp on the small nightstand and switching it on.

"Jamie."

The tortured note in his voice brought her out of her lovely haze. "What is it?"

"Sweetheart, you only had two glasses of wine. I had no idea you'd become intoxicated on so little—"

She laid her fingers over his mouth to stop his words. "It isn't the wine," she said, turning her head to meet his eyes steadily. "It's you. I'm drunk on you. I've been sober for so long, and now I can't—"

Words failing her, she lifted her arms to him. He bent to her, taking her lips hungrily, his hand parting her jacket and slipping under the tiny strap to give his palm the full sensual treat of silky skin. Lifting his mouth a fraction, he murmured, "Women must wear dresses like this to torture men. All evening I've been wondering what this dress looked like underneath that primly proper jacket. Why didn't you take it off before? Your shoulders are beautiful."

"I didn't take off my jacket for the same reason you didn't dance with me. I didn't want to do it in public, I wanted to wait until we were alone...."

His eyes gleamed with sensual pleasure at her words. "Both of us showing good sense for once. Hard to believe," he breathed, his mouth tracing the length of her collarbone, his tongue teasing around the tiny strap. "We're alone now. Raise up and let me help you...."

With expert hands he lifted the jacket away from her and tossed it behind him. When he looked back at her, his breathing seemed to stop. "You are ... exquisite." He cupped both shoulders in his hands and leaned over her to trace the sensitive hollow of her throat with his tongue. A tremor shook her, traveling along the surface of her skin and centering low and deep in her abdomen, making her aware of her desire for him. Slowly, so very slowly, he inserted his fingers under the delicate straps and nudged them over her shoulders.

"There's a zipper. In the back."

"I know." He sounded amused. "Don't rush me, sweetheart. We have time."

She might have been embarrassed, but he didn't give her the chance. He kissed her again, this time deeply and fully, claiming her with his tongue in thrusts that were meant to do exactly what they did, remind her of that more intimate, final union. Under the spell of Blake's mouth and hands, an insidious hunger was building, a need for more and more and more.

He showed no inclination to hurry. He caressed her repeatedly, sliding her silken dress against her body and her nylon-clad thighs, finding new ways to incite her to madness. She wasn't sure which gave her the most pleasure, his hands running over her hips, her thighs, her calves, the soles of her feet, or the feel of his body bent over hers, his heady male scent filling her nose, the corners of his suit jacket brushing her. She writhed in a restless attempt to free herself of the silken web he wove around her, but there was no escaping the spiral of desire winding higher and higher within her.

"Lift, Jamie. Let me ..."

The zipper separated, and the tiny straps glided down her arms and over her wrists. She arched her hips, and the dress was gone. He didn't need to be told she wore a front-hook bra. He dispensed with it and the bit of lace at her hips as easily as he had her inhibitions.

Had she thought his caresses were driving her mad before? Now she learned what madness he was capable of arousing within her. The barrier of clothing gone, he was no longer restricted to using his hands. Now he used his lips and tongue to explore the soft mounds of her breasts, the indentation of her navel, the curve of her inner thigh. Soft moans escaped her throat. He murmured encouragement to her, outrageous, wonderful words of praise. She arched her hips toward his, her body instinctively seeking the source of satisfaction.

"Aren't you forgetting something?"

The deep, sensual throatiness of his voice was like velvet drawn across her skin.

Blake looked down at her, feeling as if he were gazing at heaven. Never had he been with a woman who was more beautiful or more responsive. She was sleek and lovely, her skin like cream, her hair like silk. He wanted to possess her . . . and have her possess him.

Her need for him acted like a goad. He'd vowed to go slowly, and he'd known the only way to ensure that he did was to postpone his own undressing until the last minute. But for him, the last minute had come. He needed her more than he could ever remember needing another woman in his life. He wanted her to touch him, to run those slender fingers over his body and discover his secrets just as he'd discovered hers.

"Undress me, Jamie," he ordered her huskily.

She seemed, to his utter amazement, shy at first. Then, as the buttons of his shirt gave, as his jacket followed his vest to the floor and his tanned skin came into the light, she seemed to lose her shyness. There was a moment of awkwardness as they both forgot about the buttons on the cuffs of his shirt, and another as her slender fingers trembled over his belt buckle until, no longer able to contain his impatience, he took over the task.

He stood to undress, watching her eyes in the soft light as he emerged finally from his clothes. Something he saw there made him sit down on the bed and look at her steadily. "Jamie . . ."

Her eyes not meeting his, she reached out tentatively and touched her fingers to his nipples. She felt them change, hardening in response. "Jamie . . ."

Her hands wandered lower, exploring, touching smooth, velvet soft skin. "You are wonderful," she whispered.

His control gone, he made a muffled sound and moved over her, joining her body with his.

"I don't want to disappoint you by going too quickly."

"You won't . . . you won't disappoint me . . . unless you stop. . . ."

In loving, he was as in living, considerate, gentle, seeking her pleasure before his own, until he saw that the heat was rising in her. Just as she thought she would be consumed, he groaned and joined her in the flames.

"I WANT TO SPEND the rest of the night with you, sleep with you," Blake murmured, "but I can't."

Letting her fingertips drift over his chest, Jamie said the words she had to say. "It's all right. I understand." She let her hand drift lower, loving the way his muscles tightened under her touch, her fingers tracing a path down his arm to his wrist.

"Do you realize how often you say those words to me?" He captured her questing fingers in one smooth move, shackling her hands together.

"No, I didn't—"

"Do you understand that I'm not going to leave you . . . not just yet?" He lowered his head and brushed his mouth over a dusky nipple.

"Yes. Yes."

JAMIE LAY IN BED, the light sheet Blake had pulled over her bare body covering her as she watched him dress.

Lacking only his suit jacket and his shoes, he turned to her. "It's not supposed to be interesting to watch me put my clothes back on."

"It's interesting watching you do anything."

He sat down on the bed next to her. Her hair was tousled from his hands, her skin rosy from his loving, her lips swollen from his kissing. The need to possess rose in him like a tide. His. She was his.

Yet once before he had thought he'd found love. And it had shriveled and died under the grind of daily living. What he had with Jamie was twice as soul shaking as anything he'd shared with Kim. Would it fade twice as quickly? Jamie was young and idealistic, not nearly as tough and practical as Kim had been.

The truth that he wouldn't admit was there in front of his eyes. If he married this woman, lived with her as his wife and she changed her mind about loving him, he wouldn't survive.

Stunned, he didn't move. He'd never meant to give her such power. Yet he'd known instinctively, right from the first, that if any woman could destroy him, it was this idealistic woman who looked like an angel and made love like a wanton. He stood up to go, and discovered he was still holding her hand. "I'll call you tomorrow," he said softly.

"All right."

Unable to stop himself, he bent over and brushed his lips to hers. "Have a good sleep, Beauty." Before he could lift himself away, she caught his face in her hands. With infinite care she turned his cheek and pressed her lips against his scarred flesh. "I love you, Blake."

She didn't love him—she loved her own idealistic dream of him. He stood very still, watching her in the light pooled on her pillow. Her chestnut hair lay like gilded satin around her head. God help him, if he didn't leave soon, he wouldn't go at all . . . ever. "Good night, Jamie."

WHEN THE PHONE RANG the next evening, Jamie snatched it up eagerly. The restrained quality of Blake's voice instantly put her on guard. And later, when she put the phone down after listening to him explain he was needed on the ranch to look for the men who were stealing his cattle, she told herself there was nothing wrong, that everything would be all right between them . . . but she didn't believe it.

HE CALLED HER ONCE AGAIN, the next night. She'd already gone to sleep, and she was only half-awake when she answered the phone. The cool tone of his voice brought her quickly to consciousness, and the inconsequential things he said, and the offhand way he told her good-night kept her awake for several hours afterward.

JAMIE DIDN'T SEE BLAKE again until the night of the open house. When he walked in the door with Jenny, wearing the same suit he'd worn the night he'd gone out with her, Jamie's hand shook with reaction. She wrapped her arms around her waist and tried to concentrate on the chattering of Jennifer Clark's mother. But out of the corner of her eye she managed to keep track of Blake as he roved around the room, guided by an excited, bright-eyed Jenny.

Why hadn't he come over to say hello?

He might not be looking at her, but he certainly didn't miss anything else. He gazed at the spider plant her eager-beaver helpers had managed to overwater and nearly kill. He saw the chalk-logged erasers that neither the electric cleaner nor twenty willing children could clean. He studied the hamster as if he'd never seen a furry, four-footed creature before. He gave each of the other children's clay creations the solemn examination of an art critic. And he moved so well while he did it. And looked so good. She remembered how he'd looked emerging from that suit, his body golden in the light. . . .

He turned and caught her looking at him. With Jenny trailing behind him, he moved toward Jamie.

"Hello, Miss Gordon."

His formality chilled her. "It's nice to see you, Mr. Lindstrom." Her voice was equally cool, equally formal. Whatever game he was playing, all she could do was take his lead. "Did you find the men who were stealing your cattle?"

"Yes, we did. They've been taken over to the county seat and offered lodging." He smiled, but there was nothing in his face or eyes but polite friendliness. He was retreating behind his mask. She couldn't bear to stand there and look at him, knowing that what they had shared meant so little to him.

"Excuse me, won't you? I see another parent I should speak to."

She wanted him to leave her room, willed him to leave. He didn't, and his presence caused more trouble in addition to the ache in Jamie's heart.

Parents trying so hard to look interested and just barely disguising their boredom came alive with shock. They would look at Blake, then at the sculpture. Instantly their faces would straighten as if they feared a hidden camera. And all the while Blake remained in her room as if to confirm the likeness.

When Blake had finally left and the room had cleared of parents and children, Jamie breathed a sigh of relief and rotated her shoulders, trying to release the tension in her back. Her time of relaxation was short-lived. Tom Coachman appeared in her door. Walking in, he went straight to the table, looked at Jenny's sculpture and then turned to stare at Jamie.

"I didn't think it could be true. I hoped it wasn't."

Jamie watched him and said nothing.

"Is there some reason you've purposely subjected a member of this community to ridicule?"

She looked at him levelly. "Ridicule is in the eye of the beholder."

"If I get a call on this from one single parent . . ."

"I can't see any reason why you should."

"Perhaps you can't. I can think of a thousand. And I'll probably hear them all when my phone starts ringing off the wall Monday morning. Thank God it's our last week."

AFTER A WEEK that was so hectic that Jamie hardly had time to think about anything, Friday arrived. It was a half day, and at noon, after she'd handed out report cards, the children were gone and the building echoed with quiet.

She sat down at her desk and was thinking about her lunch with Tiki when she received a message that Mr. Coachman wanted to see her in his office.

He offered her a chair, sat down rather nervously in his and said it quickly, like a man facing the dentist's drill.

He was sorry, but she wouldn't be offered a contract for the coming year. He'd received not one but a dozen calls. People were upset. They felt Blake had been through enough, that he shouldn't have been subjected to this added embarrassment.

Having delivered the blow, Mr. Coachman relaxed back in the chair. "One caller told me you rode your horse out to the ranch to see Blake at the same time some woman reporter from New York was visiting him. She suggested you might be trying to get some publicity for yourself out of this. And your landlady tells me you laughed at him and called him a beast."

"It was a joke," Jamie said huskily.

Coachman raised an eyebrow. "Was the sculpture your idea of a joke?" At the look on her face, he shook his head. "Jamie, I know you've done a good job teaching, for the most part."

Let us not forget the faint praise that goes with damnation.

"But I simply can't ignore the animosity you've stirred up in this community. One mother told me that if her child were going to be in your classroom next year, she'd transfer him to another school. I can't have people start thinking that. This school is fighting for its life. I've got to work with the community." He sighed and pushed back a strand of thin hair. "Everyone here likes Blake. They don't want to see him hurt any more than he has been already."

Jamie felt drained. She rose from her chair. "The funny part of it is . . . I couldn't agree more."

9

BLAKE JOUNCED ALONG in the pickup toward the south range, the salt blocks sliding in the bed of the truck as he drove over the bumpy ground. It was a sparkling Saturday morning, the kind he liked best, with a wild blue sky. As he hadn't before his capture, he felt the endless sweep of prairie sky from horizon to horizon over his head.

Best of all, Jenny had had a good night last night. He'd made progress with her the other evening, and now that summer vacation had arrived, Jenny was gradually forgetting her fear that Blake would disappear again. This morning, when he'd told her he was going out to deliver salt to the stock and that he'd be back in time to eat lunch with her, she'd simply nodded and said goodbye.

Rain. When had they ever had so much rain?

Everything was wet. The bunk feeders were soaked, stained dark gray from excess water. Rain and Jamie. Two unrelated things, inexplicably linked forever in his mind.

Jamie. He couldn't stop thinking about her. Soon, very soon, he was going to have to do something about her. He had wanted time . . . but this week since he'd stayed away from her had seemed like an eternity.

Blake climbed out of the pickup, frowning. In the heat he'd stripped off his shirt, leaving his chest bare, but he still wasn't cool. Around his waist and thighs, his jeans clung, damp with perspiration. Once they'd been wet, and he'd taken them off to dry. . . .

Blue eyes came into his mind, expressive eyes and satin skin and chestnut hair as soft and shiny as silk, piled up, baring her sweet nape, or spread across a pillow....

Sweet, honest, loving woman. She was all of those. She had kept her word about displaying Jenny's work. It couldn't have been easy for her. He had tried to stay in the room and stave off any comments people might make, and he thought for the most part he'd been successful. It really hadn't occurred to him how interested other people would be in his daughter's creation . . . or how much Jamie was risking by displaying it. Several other things hadn't occurred to him. It hadn't occurred to him what torture it would be to watch her move around the room, knowing that under that proper suit was a slim body capable of such wild responsiveness....

He wrestled a block of salt out of the pickup with his gloved hands and dropped it on the ground. Cattle crowded around him, pink tongues coming out to lick the treat, their russet backs shiny, their earthy smell a balm to his soul.

He needed a balm. He needed . . . Jamie. In the press of people they hadn't been able to exchange more than a few polite words. He'd wanted to talk to her. She'd looked drawn, subdued. She hadn't looked like the woman with the nerve to jump up on a corral fence and kiss him. She had been cool to him, and he'd wondered whether it was because there were other people around...or whether her idealistic passion for him was already cooling.

The thought made sweat stand out on his forehead. Tipping his hat back and wiping his brow with his red kerchief, he forced his thoughts away from Jamie and looked at the sky, wondering if the weatherman's prediction was right and they were going to get more rain.

A horse and rider appeared on the horizon, coming his way, hell-bent for leather. The rider was taking his horse over the range with a careless disregard for the horse's safety or his own. Blake tensed, bracing himself for trouble. This rider meant business, and it wasn't Jed or any of his men.

His tension increased when he saw who it was. Drew, who hadn't been on the back of a horse since he'd left home eleven years ago. Nor, in living memory, had he been up before ten o'clock, except on mornings when he taught school. Whatever it was Drew had on his mind, it couldn't be good.

Blake straightened, a gloved hand sliding down his thigh.

Pounding up to him, Drew reined in his horse.

The contrast between them had never been more pronounced. Drew's bright golden hair was disheveled, his face harsh with emotion. Blake stood quiet as stone, his dark hair as smooth as his features, waiting, watching, like a puma biding its time before the kill. Blake pushed a cow rump and came out from behind his stock. "Hello, Drew."

Drew swung out of the saddle and advanced on Blake, aggression in his walk, his body, his eyes. Blake's body tightened in readiness. He sensed that after spending a lifetime avoiding a physical confrontation with him, Drew was closing in for the kill.

"For years," Drew said through gritted teeth, "I've resisted the urge to beat the hell out of you because I didn't want to give my father the satisfaction of seeing us at each other's throat."

"A wise decision," murmured Blake.

"But right now," Drew went on as if Blake hadn't spoken, "I don't give a damn about my father or anything else. All I can think about is how much I want to pound you to a bloody pulp." Drew's eyes were contemptuous, challenging.

Blake didn't know what he'd done to earn that contempt. He only knew he didn't like it. Slowly he removed his leather work gloves and laid them in the feed bunk. His hands as bare as his chest, he stood loosely, his arms hanging at his sides. "Don't hold back on my account."

Even though he was expecting the blow, the speed of Drew's fist caught Blake unaware. He took a crack on the jaw that reverberated through his skull like a sledgehammer and threw him backward against the empty feed bunk. Drew advanced, but his advantage of surprise was gone. Blake bounced off the bunk, blocked Drew's oncoming fist with an iron-hard arm and landed a blow to Drew's jaw. He followed it with another jab to his solar plexus. Drew's eyes went blank with surprise. He sagged to the ground and sat there, stunned.

"My God," he said between gasps. "It looks easier than that in the movies."

"It is. They don't actually hit each other."

Blake turned to the stock tank, stood over it for a minute and then braced himself and plunged his head in. He emerged dripping, shaking the excess moisture from his hair. When he'd wiped the water out of his eyes, he picked up an empty can and filled it.

Drew sat with his head over his bent knee, his eyes closed, his head down, his breathing ragged. Blake emptied the can over Drew's head.

"Cut it out! I'm not dying." Drew glared up at him, as angry as a doused cat.

Blake stared down at him, unmoved by his protest but still breathing a little hard. "If . . . it wouldn't be too much to ask, what did I do to deserve this?"

Drew sat for a moment, then shook his head. "I thought I was going to punch some sense into that stupid head of yours. I thought that just once I might make you think about somebody else besides yourself. . . ." Blood trickled from Drew's lip. He lifted a hand and wiped it away, an expression of disgust on his face.

"What are you talking about?"

Resting his forehead on his knees, Drew said in a muffled voice between breaths, "Jamie. I'm talking about Jamie." He lifted his eyes and stared at Blake and his voice, coming through pants, raised, cracked. "Dammit, man, she's lost her job. And all because of your muleheaded stubbornness and your egotistical blindness and your damn fool pride—"

"Don't waste your breath enumerating my sins. What about Jamie?"

Drew shook his head and then winced at the pain of moving. "Good God, man, despite everything, I always thought you had a level head on your shoulders. Aren't there any brains left inside that hard skull of yours at all, or did all the publicity get to you? Didn't it ever once occur to you that you were putting her job in jeopardy?"

Now it was Blake who looked dazed. "How did I . . . do that?"

Drew's mouth curled in derision. "Are you surprised? What exactly did you think would happen when you made her promise to put that damned concoction of your daughter's on display?"

"What has Jenny's work got to do with Jamie's job?"

"If nothing else, your sojourn as a hostage should have made you aware of the politics of this world. Believe me, they don't stop at the Dakota border. Coachman is afraid of losing his school, and if it comes to a choice between losing a teacher and losing a school, you can bet which one he's going to pick. Being a good teacher doesn't mean a thing if the community turns against you. And that's what has happened to Jamie, thanks to you."

For several long minutes Blake stared at Drew. "You're sure?"

"I just talked to Elaine, Coachman's secretary. Jamie's not being offered a contract for next year because the community thinks she set you up to ridicule."

"He can't do that—"

"He can do it, man, and he's done it. I tried to talk him out of it, but I couldn't. I thought I was coming out here to give you a beating because of Jamie, but maybe I just didn't like admitting defeat and coming to you for help. But I had to. Only you can straighten out this mess. I turn it over to your capable hands, Cousin." Drew was silent for a moment. "And are they capable. I hate to admit it, but you're a damned good man in a stand-up fight."

Blake paused for a long moment, his eyes meeting his cousin's. The contempt in Drew's was gone. In its place was a wary respect. "You're not so bad yourself, Cousin. Next time—" he tried to smile, but it hurt too much "—let's fight on the same side."

Drew hesitated, then put his hand in Blake's. "I'd like that a whole lot better." Drew peered at him, the cut on his mouth making him smile crookedly. "Now that we've kissed and made up, are you going to stand there all morning, or are you going to get cleaned up and go in and talk to Coachman?"

FOR THE SECOND TIME THAT MORNING, Blake was balling his fists. He was sitting in Coachman's living room, trying to ignore the man's look of polite horror at Blake's scarred face, which was beginning to swell.

"It's good of you to come here to do the gallant thing and speak up in her defense," Coachman told Blake in a patronizing tone that set his teeth on edge. "But there's nothing I can do at this point. Jamie used bad judgment in displaying the sculpture. The people of this community felt, rightfully so, in my opinion, that it was a mistake. Whatever you might have said to her, the decision was ultimately hers."

"The decision was not hers. I took it away from her by forcing her to give her word to show the sculpture before she'd even seen it—"

Coachman shook his head. "There was still time, after she'd seen it, to change her mind, and that was what she should have done." He paused and said heavily, "What a teacher exercising good judgment would have done. I'm afraid the firing must stand."

Blake rose from the chair that faced Coachman's, his head aching. He was wasting his time. "I wonder," Blake said, his face expressionless, "what the people of this community will think of your decision when they learn the truth of this matter. Perhaps they'll discover that they've placed a man in charge of their children who makes biased decisions and is intractable about changing them for fear he might lose face."

The threat hit home. Coachman's face reddened, and he began to sputter. "Now see here, Mr. Lindstrom, I've been trying to protect you from—"

"I suggest," Blake said in a voice like velvet over steel, "you start thinking about protecting yourself."

MRS. FAIRFAX WAS WORKING in her flower bed . . . and Jamie was gone. "She left early this morning," the woman told him primly, holding her battered straw hat with one gloved hand as she knelt in the pansy bed. "I don't know where she went. She didn't say. All she said was that she'd arrange to have her things moved by the end of the month."

Pain twisted through Blake. "Thank you, Mrs. Fairfax."

The woman frowned at him for a moment; then her mood changed. "I was always going to call and thank you for helping me with my roses. They're so lovely now. Could I give you a few?"

He didn't want to think about roses now. He had to find someone who knew where Jamie had gone. "I really don't have time—"

"It won't take but a minute for me to clip you a few." And before he could protest again, she'd brought a pair of shears from her workbasket.

He waited impatiently while she cut the flowers, two long-stemmed beauties, one red, one white, and then went back into the house to dampen them and wrap them in paper. By the time she finally handed them to Blake, he could hardly conceal his impatience. He thanked her for them and strode back to his car.

Bill Halbrook's pickup sat in front of Tiki's trailer house. Not caring if he was interrupting a tête-à-tête, Blake banged on the door. After a long wait Tiki answered his knock, her face flushed, even though a blast of cool, conditioned air poured from the door.

He didn't waste time. "Where is she?"

Tiki studied his bruised face with a child's curiosity. "You look terrible. What happened to you?"

"Never mind. Just tell me where she is."

Looking at him thoughtfully, Tiki said, "Are you a friend or a foe?"

"Friend, dammit. I've never been anything else. Now where is she?"

Tiki hesitated, than said rather reluctantly, "She went to Tynburn. There's a small rodeo there, and she plans to compete." She squinted up at him. "Are you sure you're her friend?"

She was talking to his back. He was gone.

10

TYNBURN LAY a hundred and ten miles northwest of Rock Falls, but it wasn't any drier there. The arena looked like a sea of mud. There'd been talk of canceling the rodeo, but in the end the decision had been made to go ahead. Jamie looked at the brown-clay goo inside the arena and felt a distinct pang of sympathy for the cowboys who were competing on the bulls and broncos. There was more falling than riding in those events, and the men would be diving into that sea of mud every time they fell. The roping events would be just as difficult. The mud would make the steers slip and slide, and the ropers' timing would be thrown off.

But rodeo men and women were a stoic lot. Most of them shrugged and said that was the way rodeoing was, dust one day and mud the next.

Jamie trailered Strawberry into the area behind the arena reserved for contestants. There'd been an attempt, as always; to create a straw cover on the ground, but the yellow strands had already been covered by the wet earth.

Conscious of the cowboys watching her to check out her driving skills, and other possible assets, Jamie backed the trailer around and maneuvered it into a spot with the ease that marked her as a seasoned competitor. She got out of the car, running her hands down her jeans to ease thigh muscles complaining about two hours of sitting, aware again of the casual but assessing glances thrown her way. She knew several of the men. The rodeo circuit was like a family reunion. The same faces kept turning up, but there were a few who were strangers to her.

Strawberry had been on the road just as long as she had and was probably just as stiff. Jamie ducked into the trailer to bring out the mare, tethered her to the side and went in search of water. After she'd filled a bucket and hauled it back to the horse, she stood and watched Strawberry enjoy her drink in slurpy pleasure.

A few minutes later, with the bridle and halter on the horse, Jamie mounted Strawberry's bare back and headed for the field set aside for cantering exercise.

It was a monotonously familiar thing to ride Strawberry back to the trailer an hour later, bring out the hay bag, fasten it to the hook on the side of the wagon and head for the pump to stand in line, waiting to refill the mare's water bucket. There were the same responsibilities every year in each new town: a level place for the trailer, water and food for Strawberry, water and food and a place to stay for her. She'd made reservations at the local motel and checked in there before she'd driven to the rodeo grounds.

"Hey, Short Stuff."

The only man in the world who called her that was Holt Edwards. The lanky cowboy came striding across the straw-covered mud toward her. "Glad to see you made it. Hey, do you think it'll rain? We sure could use some."

"Hello, Holt. Good to see you. How's Carol?" Smiling, she held out her hand to him.

He took it, his callused palm rasping against hers. "Fine, higher than a kite, waiting for our adopted baby. That's why she stayed home. The agency is supposed to call any day now."

"Congratulations," Jamie said, wondering why she should feel a little pang of jealousy, thinking of Carol's shy devotion to Holt and how lucky they both were. "If you have a girl, you'll name her Shorty after me, won't you?"

She looked up at Holt, all innocence. Holt laughed. "Naw, it's a boy, and Carol's already got a name picked out. Will you join me and the gang at supper tonight? We've found a place where we think the food is edible, if you chase it with enough black coffee."

The teasing, the friendship and the raillery of Holt's gang would ease the clenched stomach and the jittery nerves that Jamie always had before she competed. "I'd love to. Just let me know when you're leaving."

Two hours later she was sitting at a big round table, the lone female in the company of seven men, listening to them talk rodeo.

"Man, my horse stopped so short, I spun right around in that saddle like a top...."

"Did you see those bulls? They might not be sons of Satan, but they sure gotta be some shirttail relation...."

"My sister is real unhappy. Last rodeo she was at, her time was two-tenths of a second behind the gal in third place...."

"Hey, Shorty!" Holt shouted. "You gonna give us a good run tonight?"

"I can give you a good run any night, Holt," she shot back.

The men at the table burst out laughing and Jamie, only realizing the double meaning after she'd heard the words come out of her mouth, her face flaming red, turned slightly...and saw Blake standing in front of the table, staring at her.

She stared back. His face was bruised, one cheek a lovely shade of purple. He looked as if he'd been fighting. Who had his sparring partner been? Other than his face, he seemed as contained as ever, dressed in dark blue denims and a blue plaid shirt.

She swallowed, her throat tight. "Blake? What happened to you?"

"I was the recipient of a message, something a man had to say to me about you. Why didn't you tell me you might lose your job if you kept your promise to me?"

Drew. He'd been brawling with Drew. She didn't know which one of those two proud Viking men was the most irritating. "It wasn't your concern—"

"It *was* my concern." The tone of his voice made every one of those seven males at the table look up at him. Blake clamped his lips together.

"You shouldn't be here," Jamie said, wishing he hadn't come, wishing he wasn't standing there looking so aloof. "Jenny will worry."

He shifted his gaze from her to Holt, examining the arm Holt had thrown over the back of her chair. Obviously he thought she was trying to get rid of him because she was with Holt. It should have been funny, but it wasn't.

"That's why I wasn't here earlier. I'd promised to have lunch with her. Afterward we talked about how important it was that I come and see you, and she agreed. You're important to her."

"I know. I care for her, too."

She waited, breath held. It wasn't the right place or time, but Blake looked as if he were on the verge of...something.

Holt broke the silence. "Hey, honey." He gave her shoulder a friendly squeeze. "Are you gonna introduce us?"

Holt's joviality was like a dash of cold water over Jamie's head, and the look on Blake's face turned the water into an iceberg. Blake said, "That's not necessary. We've met before. In the lawyer's office in Sioux Falls last fall."

Blake was talking to Holt, but he was looking at Jamie. "You and your wife were coming out just as I was going in."

Unabashed, Holt said, "Sure, I remember now. We had gone to see about our adoption. I just didn't . . . recognize you."

Blake smiled, but it was the smile of a cobra. "Don't give it a thought."

"Sir? Would you like a table?" A waitress had intervened and stood beside Blake with that familiar half embarrassed, half pitying look.

"Why don't you join us?" Holt asked amiably.

Blake ran his eyes over Jamie in a long, excruciatingly thorough examination. "I wouldn't want to interfere." Blake dragged his gaze away from Jamie to give the waitress a chilly nod. "Lead the way."

He followed the young woman to a window table that was well within Jamie's vision, and for the rest of the meal she was forced to sit there and watch him watch her. Had he thought she didn't know Holt was married? She didn't know whether to laugh or get blazing mad. If Blake Lindstrom had stopped to think a minute, he'd have realized that if she was acquainted with Holt, she also knew his wife. Many of the men on the rodeo circuit were family men, and the majority of the women and children came along. Sometimes the wives and children competed, the sons in the junior bull riding, the wives and daughters in the barrel racing. It wasn't unusual to see a cowboy standing next to the practice field holding an infant in his arms while his wife exercised her horse.

After a length of time roughly the equivalent of an eternity, she left the restaurant, following Holt. Outside, climbing into his truck, Jamie felt Blake's eyes on her. He had turned his head and was watching her through the window. Thinking. Thinking what? That he'd caused her to lose her job and he was sorry?

Well, now the shoe was on the other foot. *Forget it, Blake. I don't need your sympathy any more than you needed mine, so don't sit around and worry about me. I'm not your responsibility. Goodbye, Blake. See you around.*

FINE, BRAVE WORDS. But two hours later, mounted on Strawberry she looked up into the bleachers surrounding the arena, and all her fine, brave words vanished like smoke. He was there, all arrogant one hundred and ninety pounds of him, perched on the highest seat, his hat drawn low over his brow in a useless attempt to hide his bruised face. Once more she was caught between laughter and tears. How could a man who looked as though he'd been through the biggest barroom brawl this side of the Rockies manage to sit there looking as if he were the king of the mountain?

He may be king, but he's a lonely monarch.

Jamie clutched the reins nervously, the leather straps binding on her palms. Strawberry responded by whickering, twisting her head toward Jamie's leg for assurance. Jamie gave it instantly. "It's all right, girl. It's all right." It wasn't all right, of course, and wouldn't be all right, but for the moment she had to hide her distress from Strawberry if she could.

She closed her eyes and tried to breathe deeply. She reached for concentration, going deep inside her mind, striving to forget everything but that liquid, floating sensation that told her she was seated properly in the saddle.

The woman competing ahead of her finished, rode off the field and turned to listen for her time, jostling Jamie's mare as she went by. Strawberry neighed low in her throat in protest and sidestepped nervously, causing the horse behind to turn restlessly and bump into the holding-pen fence. Was this entrance gate really like Grand Central Station, or was it her nervous imagination working overtime because Blake was watching?

It was her turn. Glad to leave a place where there were too many horses too close together, Jamie urged the mare forward into the arena, and the liquid, floating sensation vanished. It felt as if Strawberry was trying to trot through glue. Jamie had ridden in the arena before the rodeo began, and she thought she'd gauged its difficulty with a fair amount of accuracy, but as slippery as it had been then, it was worse now. After the bull and bronc riding events, it had become treacherous, undependable, packed hard in some places and soft in others. Strawberry wasn't skittish, but her tensed muscles under Jamie's thighs made it obvious that the horse was heading out into that unholy mass of mud with all the reluctance of any four-footed animal treading on ground where the footing was unpredictable.

"And now here she is, our schoolteacher from Rock Falls on her strawberry roan. A real big welcome for Jamie Gordon, ladies and gentlemen."

She took the mare into the arena slowly, and the cheering, the clapping, the lights receded. There was only the mud and those barrels.

She brought Strawberry around in the traditional circle to face away from the crowd. Jamie took her time, holding the mare steady, crooning to her in a low, breathy murmur, assuring her that everything was all right. Getting ready, she took a deep breath, tightened her thighs and shouted the signal to go. Strawberry whirled and took off, fighting valiantly to deliver the speed Jamie wanted.

Jamie's hat flew off, and the wind made her eyes blur with tears. Under her, Strawberry strained to pick up speed in the mud. Round the right barrel they went to do the first loop of the figure eight. With the wind and the tears in her eyes, she could hardly see. She circled the second barrel, finishing the figure eight and heading for the top of the triangle. She was moving by instinct now, her cries urging Strawberry on. Then they were around the top barrel and into the straightaway, the only place she could make up for lost time.

"Hi, hi—ya," she cried, slapping the mare with her hand. "Go, girl."

Out of the corner of her eye, she saw the red flag drop. It was over. Strawberry had performed like a champion. Jamie patted the mare and told her how wonderful she was. Mud from her elegant knees to her underside, the mare responded to Jamie's voice with a proud bob of her head.

Jamie acknowledged the crowd's applause, unable to look in Blake's direction. She rode through the gate and out of the arena, turning to listen for her time.

There was a delay. Then the announcer's voice said, "Sixteen point five. Let's give that little lady a big hand. That puts her in first place."

She didn't expect to maintain her lead. There were several women yet to compete. Even so, she was satisfied with her run. She'd done well, considering the mud. Anxious to be out of the way of the next two contestants lined up outside the gate, she patted Strawberry's side and wheeled her to head for the trailer.

A dark form emerged from the shadows by the stock pen. Blake. His sudden appearance spooked a nervous mount. The rider, a young girl, startled by a shadowy ghost in a space she thought empty of people, emitted a muffled scream. Her horse reared in fright, flailing with his hooves. Jamie grasped desperately at Strawberry's reins to ride her out of the way, but she was too late. The rearing horse's hoof caught her on the arm. The shock of having her flesh torn apart by a metal horseshoe, driven by the steel-piston precision of a panicked horse's leg, made her lose her balance and go down under the flying hooves.

Blake dived under the screaming girl's horse and leaned over Jamie, rounding his shoulders and bunching up the muscles there, making a protective arch over her, fending off the flying hooves until he could pick her up and carry her to safety. To the girl he shouted, "Get that animal the hell out of here!"

His heart pounding with shock and fear, he plucked Jamie up from the wet ground and straightened, cradling her in his arms like a child. "Somebody call that ambulance." He'd seen it, parked and ready behind the arena, knew it was there for those who competed on the bulls and broncs. Never had he thought he would be lifting Jamie onto the stretcher to watch her be borne away inside.

When the ambulance roared off, Blake, his head down, strode to where Strawberry stood trembling. He picked up the reins and led the frightened horse back to the trailer parked behind Jamie's car. He was soothing the horse when Holt caught up with him.

"Here," he said, thrusting a muddied white hat into Blake's hands. "I figured you'd want to take this to her. And I'll take care of her horse."

In the dark, Blake couldn't see the man's eyes. "Thanks," he said, his voice not quite steady. "I'll see that she gets it." He laid the hat carefully on top of the newspaper bundle in his car.

JAMIE WOKE TO AN ARGUMENT. A female voice was saying, "Sir, you really can't come in here—"

A growled reply. "It will take somebody bigger than you to keep me out."

"I'll have to speak to the doctor—"

"You do that. Then maybe he'll get his tail in here and get something done for her."

"I have to clean her up first—"

"And I'll help."

"We really feel it's better if the family stays outside until the doctor has seen the patient—"

"Why? Because they might faint and clutter up the floor? I've castrated too many calves to faint at the sight of torn flesh. Here, hand me that basin."

There was a muffled sound, a gulp of shock.

That man did use heavy artillery.

One hand picked up her wrist to take her pulse while another pair of cool, gentle hands rolled up the sleeve of her blouse, wiped her hands and face with a cool cloth, stroked her hair. Masculine hands. Blake's hands. Jamie's heart kicked into overdrive.

"Her pulse seems to be erratic—"

"Then for God's sake get the doctor in here and—"

"Blake, you're causing a lot of trouble," Jamie said from under closed lids, bracing herself for the sight of his much-loved face.

When she opened her eyes, he was standing over her, looking down at her like a man who'd just seen Christmas. Yes, of course, Blake had to be standing there looking at her like that. She was at her absolute worst, mud from end to end.

Blake didn't seem to notice. "I would have caused a lot more in about a minute if you hadn't come around." He took her uninjured hand in his, his eyes infinitely worried, infinitely tender. "How are you feeling?"

"Like I've been stepped on by a horse, or run over by a train—I'm not sure which."

He studied her for a moment, and then an unfamiliar quirk tugged at his mouth. "Well, that should be easy enough to figure out. Are there hoof prints or wheel marks on that beautiful face of yours?"

He was making a joke to help her forget her pain, and if she hadn't loved him with all her heart before, she certainly did now. Did he have any idea how beautiful that purple, scarred face of *his* was and how much she wanted to drown herself in his eyes, in his body, in him?

Blake allowed himself the luxury of looking long and hard at every inch of her bedraggled, mud-spattered, wonderful face. "I don't see any wheel marks. It must have been a horse."

"That's your final opinion, Doctor?" Her fingers moved, closed around his, and her eyes clung to his face just as tenaciously.

Those emerald depths darkened, and he smiled. "It is."

"Didn't think you had a smile in you," Jamie heard the nurse say chidingly. "You sure didn't a minute ago."

"A minute ago this lady hadn't opened her eyes. Now I could smile at anybody. Even you."

The nurse harrumphed, and luckily for Blake, the doctor appeared. He did what the nurse hadn't been able to do, convinced Blake that Jamie would be much better off if he were to step outside in the hall until the arm was stitched. When Blake turned to go, Jamie saw that his shirt was torn and his back scratched. She cried out, "Blake, your back. One of the horses must have grazed you, too."

"Yes," the doctor said thoughtfully as he looked at Blake. "When I'm finished with this lady, I think you'd better step back in here and get that scratch cleaned."

Blake looked as if he was going to argue, saw the expression on Jamie's face and nodded. "Whatever you say," he muttered, and went out.

"Nurse, you can attend to that man. It's just a surface abrasion, but see to it that it's thoroughly cleaned."

The nurse looked delighted. "Oh, I will, Doctor, I will."

Jamie glanced at the nurse, humor in her eyes. "You won't use anything too potent on him, will you?"

"You heard the doctor. I have to make sure the wound is clean," the nurse said with evident enjoyment. Jamie bet she would tackle the job with a large supply of two things: enthusiasm and an antiseptic that stung like the devil.

The doctor wanted her to stay in the hospital overnight for observation, but Jamie refused. In simple truth she couldn't afford it, and she didn't think it was necessary. She felt perfectly fine except for her arm, which he'd stitched. When he saw she was determined to leave, he left her for a few minutes. When he returned he handed her a bottle of pills. "These are for pain. I've asked Mr. Lindstrom if he was able to keep an eye on you tonight, and he assured me he was more than willing to do so. If you have any blurring of vision or headaches, contact us immediately."

She had an instant blurring of vision, but it wasn't from her physical condition. Blake had volunteered to spend the night with her, but had he done it because he felt responsible or because he loved her?

Not sure she could bear spending a night with him because he felt she was an obligation he had to see through to the bitter end, she went out into the lobby to wait while Blake had his back treated.

He came out looking like a knight who'd been unseated in a tournament joust. "Come on," he said, taking her arm. "Let's get out of here."

"Are you okay?"

He grimaced. "I think so. I won't know until next year when my back stops stinging."

With the gentlest of touches that steadied and did nothing more, Blake led her to his car and helped her inside. His touch made her light-headed, giddy. Ridiculous to feel that way. The local anesthetic the doctor had used was wearing off, and her arm was beginning to throb and ache. But it seemed as if the pain belonged to another person. Perhaps Blake didn't think of her as his responsibility, after all. He'd cared enough to come to the hospital, and he'd fought to be with her. He'd stepped between the horses to protect her— Jamie sat up in the seat.

"Strawberry. I forgot all about her."

"All taken care of. Snug and sound, rubbed down and put away for the night."

Jamie relaxed back. "Thank you."

"Thank Holt. He drove your car over to the motel for you, as well."

She was grateful to Holt, but she wasn't sure when she would see the cowboy again. She seemed to be floating at a height somewhere above the earth where nothing could touch her.

11

FOR JAMIE, the floating feeling remained, even when Blake reached the motel and escorted her into her room. As he flicked on the light and she stood blinking from the brightness of it, he took something from his pocket. "The nurse suggested you might like this plastic bag to put over your arm so you could take a shower."

He walked to the table beside the bed and laid the packet down. When he turned to her, quiet permeated the room. "Would you like me to help you get cleaned up?" He looked controlled, almost indifferent. But was he? The air between them crackled with thoughts unsaid. There were questions on other levels, questions that went deep, too deep to be voiced.

He seemed to be asking silently, *Do you trust me to look at you, touch you intimately... again?*

Her eyes clung to that dark, saturnine face, wishing she could see into his mind. "Are you offering because you feel responsible for what happened?"

"I'm offering," he said in a velvety rasp, "because I... need to."

"Why, Blake? Why do you need to?" That drifting cloud was back, and she was on it, moving toward him. Or was he moving toward her?

"Jamie," he ground out harshly, but he was close enough to touch.

So she did, cupping her hands tenderly around his face and telling him, "I want your... help."

"This is wrong, all wrong," he said throatily, his face and words telling her he knew she wanted far more than his help in undressing. "You've been hurt—"

"Then don't hurt me more by pushing me away. Just . . . kiss me."

In the half-lit room he looked tortured, a man on the rack. Her body touched his, and there was infinite satisfaction in feeling the indrawn breath he took and watching the darkening of his eyes. There was even greater satisfaction in feeling his chest against her breasts, his hips cradling hers and his unmistakable arousal nudging her. "If I'm going to have that shower, Blake, you'll have to . . . help me . . . with my clothes."

Blake, feeling as if he were exploding inside, lifted his fingers to her shirt. As his hands moved down, feminine skin, soft and silky, began to emerge. Then the first, sweet curve of her breasts appeared. Then more, more of smooth, rounded flesh, until the dark budding nipples peeked through lace, flesh that he wanted to free from captivity, explore and handle and take in his mouth. He pulled her shirt from her jeans, knowing he deserved this torture, seeing the feminine beauty he had tried to forget and couldn't. It was his jealousy and carelessness that had caused her pain. While Jamie was getting ready to compete, he'd gone to Holt to find out what kind of game the man was playing. After he'd finished talking with the cowboy, he'd felt like the biggest fool in the world. He'd wanted to go to Jamie, tell her he was sorry, and that he was leaving and he wouldn't bother her again. That's why he'd been standing in the shadows. He'd been thinking only of telling her what a stupid fool he'd been so as to erase that look from her face, the one she'd worn when she'd looked back through the restaurant window at him.

When he'd seen her go down under that horse, he had thought his heart would stop. That anything should happen to her because of him . . .

And now she stood here, inviting him to make love to her. There was invitation everywhere he looked, in the touch of her hands, in her eyes, in the faint flush of her skin. She was the most generous, loving woman he had ever known, and he had no right in the world to make love to her again . . . and there was no way in hell he could keep from it.

"It . . . unhooks in the front."

She sounded shy and amused at the same time, and he realized he'd been looking for the bra clip in the back. This bit of lace that confined her breasts was blue, and its purpose was support, not cover. His hands shaking ever so slightly, he located the fastening, and it came apart in his hands. He drew the straps down, carefully lifting the string of silk over her injured arm.

The belt she was wearing and the fastening on her jeans were as familiar to him as his own. He knelt to pull off her boots, and the jeans followed. There was only one small bit of nothing left, the high-cut panties that, like her bra, revealed more than they concealed.

A fine line of chills skated under Jamie's skin and centered under her breastbone. As if he knew, he bent his head to kiss her there, and under the overhead light his face was thrown into sharp relief. Bruised on one side, harshly asymmetrical on the other, the drawn and puckered flesh like a cruel joke overlying the classically molded perfection of his head. But when the tip of his tongue touched the ultrasensitive skin between her breasts, she forgot his injury, forgot his strange neglect of her in the past few days. The light played over the dark silk of his hair. His hands slid warmly up her spine, and he was Blake again, the man her heart recognized as lover.

He drew away from her, releasing her. She gave a little sigh of regret, and he heard it. His mouth curving, he went to the table and picked up the plastic bag. "The nurse gave me strict instructions about this." He slid it over her arm, and as he looked down at the gauze-covered wound through the transparent plastic, his face changed, grew harshly self-condemning. "This happened to you because of me."

She raised her other hand to his hair and slid her fingers into the dark, silky mass. "It was an accident, Blake. If I don't blame you, why should you blame yourself?"

He gazed at her for a long moment, then turned his head and let his lips graze her inner arm. "Because it's the truth."

She went up on her toes to kiss him, brushing her lips over his, stopping his words. "Don't, Blake." At his shake of the head, she said quickly, "You're guilty of something much more serious."

He looked startled.

"You're still fully dressed. And I can't..." She raised the bagged hand, her eyes dark and full of laughter.

To Blake she was a shy Eve, secure in her beauty, aware of the tantalizing promise in her smile. His hands were unsteady as he raised them to his shirt buttons.

Golden shoulders emerged from under the blue plaid cotton, as well as a chest sprinkled with dark, crisp hair, defining nipples and traveling a path to his navel. He bent to pull off his boots and jeans, and under the copper skin, muscles moved like threads of steel. A strong man. A powerful man. But between those muscles was the beginning of the wound he had suffered because he'd put his body between her and two panicky, kicking horses. He'd thought nothing of protecting her. He insisted he wasn't a hero, but he was.

He straightened, and those darkly green, wonderfully deep eyes looked into hers, asking the question once again. *Are you sure this is what you want?*

She gave him the answer with her face and her body and her eyes. *Yes. Yes.*

With exquisite gentleness he drew her last garment from her.

The shower was slow and warm, covering her skin like balm. Blake stood behind her in the stall, his hands slippery with soap smoothing over her bare shoulders to soothe aching muscles. He found the spot under her shoulder blade that ached and rubbed it knowingly. She bent her head and sighed in utter bliss and contentment. Warm, warm, the water was warm. Blake's hands were warm and she was turning into a dark, aching flame....

Reaching under her arms, his agile fingers slid quickly and matter-of-factly over her, soaping her breasts and circling her abdomen. Her body protested his casual handling. Her skin remembered his touch, and she wanted, needed more.

His hands curled around her hipbones, no longer casual. Holding her locked in place, he lifted her hair and nipped her lightly at the nape. She forgot what she had wanted, forgot what she was, who she was. A delicious shudder began where his mouth was and rippled down her back.

He was wily, was her man, and full of surprises, denying here, delighting there. His hands glided over her femininity without a pause, while a thigh nudged provocatively against her buttock and his tongue sought along her backbone, looking for the most sensitive vertebra.

While he was soaping her thighs, he found that vertebra, low, between her hips. "Blake—"

His mouth was gone, and so was he, except for those
impersonal hands sudsing her toes.

Had she thought his hands were impersonal? Wrong,
wrong, wrong. The soap skittered to the floor of the
shower, and now those wonderful fingers explored every
bone of her ankle as if he were rediscovering the way she
was made. "Blake," she said again, her voice husky, but
whether she was asking him to stop or begging him to
continue, she didn't know. He murmured something to
her, a low, conciliatory sound of admiration and reassur-
ance. His hands trailed up over her calves and thighs, and
then higher, discovering the curve of her buttocks, finding her hipbones. He shaped her, molded her, turned her
to flame. His wrists slid around her rib cage and under her,
and her breasts were cupped lovingly in hands that knew
exactly how to touch water-slick, sensitive skin.

"Lean against me, sweetheart."

She hesitated, not because she was afraid, but because
she didn't want him to go tumbling over backward.

"It's all right," he murmured darkly. "Trust me."

For a fraction of a second his hands were still. He waited
for her to acknowledge his words, and she knew that he
was asking for more than the simple trust his question im-
plied.

Without hesitation, she did as he asked. Moist skin met
moist skin, his harder, hair-crisp body taking the weight
of her softer, smoother one. Against her back she felt the
throb of his heart, insistent, accelerated, and the quick-
ened pace of his breathing. The thing she had wished for
had somehow miraculously come true. This time she was
disturbing him as much as he was disturbing her. What a

heady sense of power to know she could elicit a response from his body as strong as the one he incited in her.

She nestled into him, her skin registering every sensation of his flesh against hers. Instinctively she tried a small, circular movement. Testing the sensual feel of skin against skin and finding it delightful, she moved again, dragging her body against his.

He breathed in sharply, his senses clamoring with the need to fill her with his body and stamp his possession on her. "I suggest you stop doing that."

Smiling, she moved again in the other direction.

"Jamie—"

The rasp of his voice was very pleasing. A chill of elation shivered over her. Steadying herself against the stall with her injured arm, she reached down for the soap. "My turn," she said, coming around to him.

Watching his face, she made sudsy circles over his chest, giving careful attention to his nipples. His flesh hardened under her fingers. She began to experiment, touching, fondling, exploring.

He had, she thought, the look of a man being told of his execution at dawn. Using the guise of soaping him, she explored his body leisurely. She gave him the same teasing treatment of his sex that he'd given hers and applied the same loving attention to his legs and feet. When his skin was covered with the soap bubbles she had applied, she urged him under the spray. He revolved obediently, but his face had taken on a look of determination that thrilled her. When his body was free of soap, he reached out and shut off the water, drew her into his arms and kissed her, a deep, intimate kiss, his tongue demanding retribution for her provocation.

Outside the shower, their bodies dry and wrapped in towels, Blake looked at her, savoring the sight of her water-silked, bare body.

She didn't move, returning his deeply absorbed gaze with her own loving look, and the sweet, agonized longing in her eyes echoed exactly what he was feeling.

No longer able to resist the sweet enticement of her, he picked her up and carried her to the bed, laying her down carefully and tucking the towel in around her. He stretched out beside her and enclosed her in his arms. She cuddled into his body, loving the feel of his legs covering hers, the weight of his hand on her rib cage.

Slowly, with infinite care, he drew the towel away and began to feather kisses over her abdomen, filling her with delighted shock. As if he knew exactly how she was feeling, he deepened his onslaught, sucking on the rounded jut of her hipbone. She was soothed and petted, teased and pleasured over and over again, her breasts touched and kissed until she lingered on the border of insensibility. He rediscovered the star-shaped beauty mark and gave it his entire concentration, murmuring against her skin while he traced around the tiny mole with his tongue. Fire licked in her veins while her skin burned and her body came alive with new and consuming needs.

He sought the source of those needs, discovering the feminine triangle and moistness that waited within. There was more exploration, more exquisitely provocative soothing. The slow, endless delight he gave her brought a moan to her lips.

"Easy, my love, easy. We have time...."

Her hand closed over his, and she whispered his name and moved her hips restlessly against him in that age-old invitation.

"Ah, sweetheart. Don't tease me like that. Not unless you mean it—"

She moved again, more recklessly this time, more demandingly.

He groaned, a low sound of surrender. His body, hard, heavy, wonderfully erotic, covered hers.

As he entered her, he kissed her hard, long and deep, drinking from her mouth as if desperate to become one with her in every way. When he began to move again, it seemed as if he had. The aching wonder of being joined with him made her want to cry out with happiness. She clung to him, filled with the sure knowledge that her body was riding with Blake to the edge of a cataclysmic storm.

MUCH LATER, in the softly lit room, his thumb found her lower lip. "Are you all right? Your arm—" His voice was love softened, flowing over her like brandy.

"I'm fine."

"You are that." He leaned over her, and his warm breath fanned her cheek. She moved restlessly, inviting him to complete the kiss. His lips fastened over hers, a possession in his mouth that hadn't been there before. His tongue nudged her lips open to explore the sweetness within as if it were his supreme right. Hard male flesh rubbed her breasts; smooth taut lips plied her with sensual pleasure. All thought of resistance gone, she arched toward him. No longer the aggressor, he moved a breath away from her face and murmured, "Jamie. Be reasonable."

"I don't want to be reasonable. I want to be loved." All wanton, she lifted her mouth to his and pressed her breasts against his hard chest. His groan of need sighed into her mouth and, against her hip, his body hardened. With a primitive possession that gave her exquisite pleasure, he claimed what she so willingly offered.

SHE WOKE to the smell of hot coffee and roses. The velvety blossoms, one red, one white, lay across the brim of a brand-new hat, a russet brown one with strings. The crown was a pinch-front, the hat band studded with turquoise beads and a sassy yellow feather. She put it on, let the strings dangle under her chin and sat up under the sheet, leaning back against the headboard and looking as saucy as the feather.

The coffee smell came from the plastic cup in Blake's hand. He stood by the bed, fully clothed, looking down at her, taking in the incongruous sight of her bare shoulders peeking above the sheet and the hat perched at a perky angle on her head, his face expressing a peculiar combination of pleasure and pain.

"What time is it?" With his eyes on her, she was aware of her body, bare and warm and tender with loving and only scantily covered by the sheet. "You've been busy. Is that rain I hear?"

Blake offered the cup he held to her. In the soft grayness of the morning light, protected from the patter of rain, she was locked in a special private world with him, the world where she'd wanted to be, she knew now, since she'd seen him walk into the airport and lift his daughter into his arms. Her heart pounding with joy at the sweet intimacy, she sipped the black liquid—and made a face.

He placed the cup on the stand and sat down on the bed beside her, a hard hip nudging her. A lazy smile tilting his lips, he lifted a finger and pushed the brim of the hat back to give him a better view of her face. "Too strong for you?"

He wasn't talking about the coffee, and she knew it. He was asking her how she was, how she felt this morning. Her eyes gleaming with laughter, she said boldly, "It was just right. Did you tell me what time it was?"

His gaze went over her, lazily cataloging her eyes, the shape of her nose, the color in her cheeks. "I thought teachers were supposed to answer questions, not ask them."

She went right on asking them. "Where did you get these? They're gorgeous." She picked up the red one and held it to her nose, breathing in the glorious scent.

"There's gorgeous . . . and gorgeous." His eyes trailed over her bare shoulders and lower, to the sweet curves hiding under the sheet. His eyes raised to hers, and the gleam in them mocked her sudden modesty. Last night he'd kissed and caressed those sweet curves until he knew every inch of them. "There ought to be a law prohibiting a woman from looking as beautiful as you do the minute you open your eyes, hair all tumbled, mouth all soft and warm."

"How do you know?" She slanted a teasing glance at him, savoring her new freedom to be his lover.

"Are you inviting me to find out?"

"I just thought you shouldn't go around making rash statements without positive proof."

He leaned over and nibbled her lips. "Just as I suspected," he murmured against her mouth. "Guilty as charged."

She breathed in the essence of him, that of a soapy-clean male mingled with the scent of toothpaste and coffee. Laying the rose beside her on the pillow, she reached for him, cupping her uninjured hand around his nape and sliding lower in the bed, taking him with her, catching him under the brim of her hat until they were sharing it. He came unresistingly, succumbing to her sweet enticement. She held him there, hovering a tantalizing breath away from her lips. "You didn't tell me where the roses and the hat came from."

"The roses came from Mrs. Fairfax's garden. The hat came from the store."

"Why did you buy me a new hat?"

"I figured the fastest lady in the rodeo deserved a new hat."

"I won?"

"You won."

"Does the winner get a kiss?"

He lifted her into his arms, and she got a true winner's kiss, sweet, dark, intimate.

She sank away from him, flushed and disturbed, wondering how it was possible for him to take her from sleepy warmth to blazing need so quickly.

Watching her, he said, "What are your plans for the next few days?"

"My plans?" The sudden coolness of his tone brought her out of her rosy haze more effectively than a dash of cold water in the face.

"If it works out with Jenny, I could arrange to get away from the ranch for a week or so," he was saying in that same dispassionate voice. "I thought we'd go to Denver for our honeymoon, or if you like, Las Vegas—"

Fully awake now, she said coolly, "What honeymoon?"

"Ours, of course."

"I don't recall your proposal...or even a declaration of love."

"Love isn't a prerequisite for marriage."

The shock came first, the hurt followed, and like streams roaring toward a river, they converged into anger. "Nor to lovemaking, either, obviously."

"What is it you want? A declaration of undying love?"

"No. Not . . . now."

He stood unmoving, as still as stone. She lay there, aware of him watching her, a peculiar expression on his face. A strange, anesthetized calm came over her, the blankness of mind and body one got when subjected to a pain too great to bear.

"Would you like some more coffee?"

"No. I'd like you to leave so that I can get ready to go."

He looked undisturbed by her request for privacy. "I'll leave my car here and drive you home. How long do you think it'll take you? Shall I meet you in the lobby in twenty minutes?"

She thought about telling him the truth, that she had no intention of going with him anywhere. Somehow it no longer seemed to matter what she said to him or what he said to her. There was only one thing that mattered. Last night had been a sham from beginning to end. "You'd better make it a half hour." How was it possible to feel such pain and still be able to think and talk?

"Perhaps I could stay and help you pack. With that arm, it might take longer."

"No. Just give me . . . ten minutes' grace."

Her refusal didn't seem to bother him in the slightest. He was the same rock-hard, stone-hearted man he'd been before last night. Her loving him had made no difference to him.

How could she marry him, loving him so much and knowing he loved her not at all? She snatched the hat off the bed and thrust it into his abdomen, making him catch his breath. "Here. Take your hat with you. Since I lost my head last night, I won't be needing it."

HE WENT. He'd give her an extra five minutes to cool off, and then he'd go back and talk to her. But when he returned to the motel, she was gone.

In the drizzling rain and the gray cloudy day, he cursed. She'd left him behind deliberately. Had she gone out alone to hook up the trailer, with that injured arm? Did she hate him so much?

Calling himself fifty kinds of a fool, Blake got into his car and raced through the streets of town to the outlying countryside where the rodeo arena stood. The yard was empty except for one blue van lingering at the gate. Holt Edwards sat inside talking to a man who wore a badge. He saw Blake and waved him to come over. Blake stood outside, water dripping down his neck.

"Have you seen Jamie?" Blake asked, his heart thudding in anxiety.

"Yup. Came in here like a hundred demons were after her, had me help her load up her horse and tore out again. Never seen a lady in such a hurry."

A severe pain rose in the region of Blake's heart. "Did she say where she was going?"

"Not to me, she didn't. Got a problem?"

Blake could see the man with the badge eyeing his scarred face curiously. "Nothing I can't solve."

SILLY TO CRY OVER A MAN. Idiotic, that's what it was, to shed tears over that hard, rock-flint man. To cap her insanity, here she was, trying to drive a car and a trailer down a slippery road with one hand when she could hardly see through the rain and her brimful eyes.

But if you could live last night all over again, would you?

Yes. Yes.

Do you regret a single minute of it?

No.

The car slid on the wet gravel, forcing Jamie to pay closer attention to her driving.

She plowed on through the grayness, hardly remembering when she'd passed through a town or the last time she'd seen a car. Sensible people stayed off soggy roads. They didn't fall in love with returned hostages, either. They had wonderfully prosaic problems like what to wear to work and how to make the next car payment. They didn't drive through the pouring rain in such a befuddled state of mind that they heard horns honking.

The car was looming up behind her, coming up much too fast in her side mirror, horn blaring like New Year's Eve.

Blake's car. Grimly she dragged her eyes away from the side mirror and stared at the road, maintaining her speed with a steady pressure on the accelerator.

He stayed behind her, swerving from side to side, laying on his horn. He'd gone insane. Stark raving mad. And if he thought his crazy stunt was going to make her stop, he had another think coming. Because if he stopped, he might talk to her, and if he talked to her, she might change her mind and marry him and go with him on a honeymoon to Denver or Las Vegas or the moon. Or wherever he wanted to go.

Blake hadn't prayed often or well in his life, but he made up for a lifetime of neglect in five minutes. If he tried to pull around her, he ran the risk of forcing her into soft gravel on the shoulder or driving into it himself and losing control. And if he lost control of his car and went into the ditch, he knew darned well she'd say good riddance and keep right on going, and he'd be lucky if he ever saw her again.

Jamie said an unladylike word under her breath. Now he was trying to pass her. She inched over to the left.

Blake gritted his teeth, gripped the wheel and honked. The horse trailer stayed in the middle of the road, blocking him.

Feeling the pull of the wet earth under the wheel, and knowing if they met another car on this rainy country road it would be big trouble for both of them, he gunned the motor and pulled alongside the trailer. Then, just as he thought he was going to slide into the ditch, she panicked and pulled over, allowing him to whip around in front of her car. With a burst of speed he pulled ahead of her, slowed enough to yank the wheel around and skidded to a stop crosswise in the road, squarely in Jamie's path.

Frozen with horror, Jamie thought her eyes were playing tricks on her. When she realized they weren't and she was aimed like a cannonball for a broadside into Blake's car, she slammed on the brakes. Metal screamed with friction, and the trailer jackknifed and rammed against the hitch.

A foot from Blake's car, she brought hers to a shuddering stop. The only thing she could hear was the slap of the windshield wipers and the ragged sound of her own breathing.

She sat there trembling like a leaf. Was the man mad? Like the wind rising, her shaking dissolved into fury that mushroomed, enveloping her in rage.

She opened the door and stomped down into the mud. He'd gotten out of his car and was walking toward her. She shoved a streamer of wet hair out of her eyes and shouted, "You could have killed us both!"

He looked like a man turned to ice. "I had nothing to lose. If you didn't care enough to stop, it wouldn't have made any difference what happened to me."

She stood dazed, hardly able to believe what she'd heard. "If...you really feel that way, why couldn't you tell me you love me?"

As if driven beyond some outer limit of control, he grabbed her and pushed her against his car, his hands like steel on her arms. But steel didn't tremble. "You don't understand—"

She lifted her hands to him, and for the first time since he'd met Jenny at the airport, she saw what she'd been looking for in his face. Pain. "Explain it to me."

The rain poured over his face and hers. Watching her eyes widen and darken, he cried, "Dammit, you're a beautiful, idealistic woman who believes in heroes and fairy tales. You don't really love me. You love your hero image of me."

Jamie raised her face to his, her eyes dark with temper. "Your hero image? You don't have a hero image."

He stood there, rain dripping around him, looking as if she'd hit him.

"If you think I've set you up as a hero, you have rocks in your head. You're arrogant and pigheaded and far too fond of having your own way. Your only redeeming feature is your love for your daughter, but if you think I'm going to marry you because you're a good father—" she was shouting now "—you're crazy!"

"Maybe I am," he said, taking a tentative, vulnerable step toward her. "Maybe I am, taking on a wildcat like you. Because if you left me . . . if I let you into my life and you walked away from me . . . I wouldn't want to live."

She was too angry with him to realize what he'd admitted. "You see? I was right. Just as I said, you're pigheaded and arrogant. What makes you think you're the only one who possesses the sterling qualities of loyalty and faithfulness? You think I don't have enough backbone to stay married to you? You just try it for a few years, buddy, and you'll see."

"I want more than a few years," he said through gritted teeth. "You say you love me now. But after the glamour wore off, after you lived with me awhile, day after day—"

"Glamour? What glamour?" She took a step closer to him, her body hot with fury under her slicker. "You stupid idiot, can't you get it through your thick skull that I love you, not because you're a hero but because you're you? Though why I had to fall for someone as mule-headed as you, I'll never know."

Blake stared at her, thinking she knew him much better than he'd thought she did.

Jamie made another swipe at her face, clearing it of water, wondering if the expression on his face was really changing or if it was her imagination because that was what she wanted so desperately to see. Steeling herself not to hope for what couldn't be, she returned to the attack, no longer caring that she'd bared her soul to him. If he was going to walk away from her, he'd at least know it wasn't her lack of love but his lack of trust that was destroying them. "You're just using my idealism as an excuse to save yourself from admitting the truth. You're a coward, Blake, and you don't know how to laugh . . . or how to love."

"I know how to love," he said through gritted teeth. "You taught me that."

Joy, hard, pervasive, euphoric, sang through her. It wasn't a full declaration, but for Blake it was surrender. She took a step toward him. "Then all we have left is the laughing. You smiled once in the rain. Maybe you can do it again. Tilt your face up to the sky—" she showed him how, shutting her eyes to keep the rain out "—and get it very wet, and then you smile. And pretty soon the smile becomes a chuckle and than a genuine laugh—"

"Forget the damned rain." He pulled her into his arms. His mouth, warm with promise, covered hers. Joyously she returned his kiss, until the brim of his hat made water drip down the back of her neck.

She sputtered away from him. "You're not paying attention. How do you expect to learn anything if you keep kissing the teacher?"

She opened her eyes...and found him gazing at her with a look that took the breath from her body, a look she was no longer imagining. He loved her. And he would go on loving her for the rest of his life, just as she would him. He said, "I don't know. I guess I'll have to go right on taking lessons. Know anything about making love in the back seat of a car?" He scooped her drenched body up in his arms.

"No. Blake, put me down—" She struggled, kicking, but her heart wasn't in the effort. He was Blake, lover, friend, soon-to-be husband. Hers.

Unperturbed by her token protest, he bore her toward the car, determination in his face and his hands. "In that case . . . we'll try a little role reversal. This time I'll be the teacher."

"Blake. I'm soaked and so are you—"

"We'll get out of our wet clothes before we catch pneumonia. As it happens, I have a sleeping bag and some blankets with me."

"Blake, Strawberry is getting restless, and I think the trailer is stuck in the mud—"

"Later," he said against her mouth. "I'll worry about practicalities later."

"*We'll* worry...together," she said, prompting him, her eyes alive with love.

"Together," he grated in final surrender, bending his head to take her mouth in the kiss that celebrated his fate.

September 19 *South Dakota Gazette*
By Pauline Brighton New York City
Blake Lindstrom walked out of the hospital today, several days after undergoing an operation to remove his facial scar. He was accompanied by Jamie Lindstrom, his bride of four months and a teacher who, after an unjust firing, was recently reinstated in the Rock Falls school district. Mrs. Lindstrom admitted to this reporter that it was largely because of her husband's efforts that her job was restored to her. "He's a very persuasive man," his wife said, smiling.

She was more forthcoming than her husband. When asked how it felt to have a new face and a new bride, Lindstrom showed that in one respect, at least, he hasn't changed since his release from the hands of terrorists five months ago. "No comment," he said, just before he helped his wife into a cab and climbed in beside her.

This month's
irresistible novels from

— TEMPTATION —

TWELVE ACROSS by Barbara Delinsky

Leah Gates made up crossword puzzles for a living, a nice tame occupation in a safe urbane setting. And *this* — knee-deep mud, lashing rain, a burned-down cabin — she knew spelled disaster. What had her friend Victoria been thinking of, sending her up here to the wilds of New Hampshire?

Woodsman Garrick Rodenhiser was stunned and wary when Leah turned up shivering on his porch. A beautiful woman, miles from nowhere, meant trouble for him. But he couldn't slam the door in her face . . . or shut out the storm of feeling that raged between them.

THE BEST THINGS IN LIFE by Rita Clay Estrada

Honey Carter was aghast to find a three-year-old abandoned in her van, the victim of an attempted kidnapping. But she was *really* surprised when the child's father came to claim her. Single parent Beau McGuire was also the lead hunk in *Tomorrow's Promise*, the nation's hottest soap!

Country-bred, practical Honey didn't know what to make of this outgoing city boy. But Beau proved to be warm, sincere . . . and totally seductive. He aroused her as no man ever had. She almost forgot all the reasons why they shouldn't become lovers. . . .

LAUGHTER IN THE RAIN by Shirley Larson

Who else but a hero could have survived the six-month ordeal Blake Lindstrom had? But if he thought schoolteacher Jamie Gordon had put him on a pedestal — he had another think coming!

She was bound to this virile rancher by more than admiration and sympathy. From very personal experience, she knew what he was made of . . . flesh and blood, passion and deep tenderness. If Jamie could only teach him to laugh again, he might let all that love inside him flow free. . . .

Spoil yourself next month
with these three novels from

—TEMPTATION—

AS TIME GOES BY by Vicki Lewis Thompson

If only Cliff Hamilton had opened his eyes ten years ago! In high school Sarah Melton had been crazy about this warm, sensitive guy, though she'd hidden her feelings. She and Cliff had been fellow history buffs, that was all. But even chaste hugs and kisses would have been better than nothing. . . .

Now, ten years later, Cliff saw "Marvellous Melton" very clearly as an exciting – and damned independent – woman. And hugs and kisses weren't enough for him. He had to convince Sarah that he was the man for her. . . .

BIRDS OF A FEATHER by Leigh Roberts

For fun, Sarabeth Connolly entered San Francisco's annual Bay-to-Breakers costume race. Running alongside her was biologist Adrien Spencer – dressed as a redwood tree, no less!

His sexy voice sent shivers up her spine and left her wondering what was under all that bark . . . When she found out, she wasn't disappointed. Dynamic and arousing, single-parent Adrien was also a wonderful father to his little son. Sarabeth couldn't quell the nesting instinct rising within her. . . .

THE FAMILY WAY by Jayne Ann Krentz

Having a baby was supposed to be a joyous occasion, but Pru Kenyon wasn't smiling. True, her relationship with live-in love Case McCord was both electrifying and deeply satisfying. But she didn't have the benefit of a ring on her finger. . . .

Pru wasn't about to force Case's hand by revealing her secret. She knew he'd propose out of a sense of duty, rather than love. And if she couldn't have his love, she didn't want him. . . .

Barbara Delinsky strikes again!

Remember Victoria Lesser, the offbeat, warmhearted widow who couldn't help meddling in her friends' lives – and love affairs?

She sent Neil and Deirdre to the same "deserted island" when they needed to get away from it all. (*The Real Thing*.)

And this month, in *Twelve Across*, she's tricked Leah into moving up north, to a cabin that has burned down three months before! Naturally Leah just *has* to take shelter with Garrick . . .

Look out for Victoria again in May when her grateful, happily-ever-after friends send her off on a romantic adventure she'll never forget. Sailing into the sunset, looking for buried treasure – surely that'll give Victoria enough to do without meddling in yet another couple's romance . . . or will it?

Don't miss

A Single Rose

coming in May from Temptation